Henry David Madge

Leaves From the Golden Legend

Henry David Madge

Leaves From the Golden Legend

ISBN/EAN: 9783337392710

Printed in Europe, USA, Canada, Australia, Japan

Cover: Foto ©Andreas Hilbeck / pixelio.de

More available books at **www.hansebooks.com**

LEAVES FROM THE
GOLDEN LEGEND

CHOSEN BY H. D. MADGE, LL.M.
WITH ILLUSTRATIONS BY
H. M. WATTS

ARCHIBALD CONSTABLE & CO.

WESTMINSTER

1898

INTRODUCTORY NOTE.

EW books once as widely known as the Golden Legend, have fallen afterwards into so great an obscurity. Three centuries of fame followed its first appearance, and now it is to be met with only in a few rare copies, the treasured possessions of antiquarians and book-lovers.

It belongs to the thirteenth century, the central epoch of the middle ages. The author, Jacobus de Voragine, was of some note in his time as a theologian, a statesman and a man of virtue. Born in 1230, at Varaggio, a small town on the Gulf of Genoa, not far from Savoy, he joined, while quite young, the recently founded Order of Friars Preachers or Dominicans and soon distinguished himself by zeal for study and holiness. When he had risen to the position of Provincial of his order in Lombardy, the Pope paid a tribute to his merits by choosing him for the grateful task

of absolving the Genoese from censures which they
had incurred by disobedience to the Holy See.
The most eventful period of his life began in
1292, when a unanimous vote of the Chapter
made him Archbishop of Genoa. He set himself
to be a peace-maker between the Guelphs and
Ghibellines, and his efforts to heal the unending
quarrel were rewarded by striking, though only
temporary, success : during the unheard-of period
of eleven months the republic enjoyed a cessation
of strife such as none even of the oldest inhabitants could remember. When the streets of the
city again became fields of battle, the good Archbishop threw himself into the midst of the com-
batants and parted them at the peril of his life.
Other prelates would often spend much of their
time at Rome, the fountain-head of promotion;
but like Chaucer's "poure persoun of a toune"
Jacobus de Voragine "dwelte at hoom and kepte
wel his folde" : he made it a rule for himself
never to leave his diocese. The lax manners or
clergy and laity engaged him in anxious endeavours
after their improvement which were the more
readily accepted because his own private life was
austere. His charity towards the needy, as we
are told, knew no limits. At the age of 68 or 69,
death ended his seven years of troubled dignity on
July 14th, 1298, and he was buried, according to
his wish, in the Dominican church of his episcopal
city.

Among the nine works which historians of his
order ascribe to him are a Chronicle of Genoa, an

account of his predecessors in the See and Sermons. But his world-wide reputation rested on a book written between 1270 and 1280 and called " Historia Longobardica sen Legenda Sanctorum," but better known by the name which admiring readers bestowed on it : The Golden Legend.

In intention it belonged to strictly religious literature and was arranged to supply a course of reading for the year in the order of the calendar. Writings, of the Fathers, Lections appointed to be read in churches, Acts of the martyrs and popular traditions supplied the material which Jacobus de Voragine compressed and abridged so as to bring the whole within reasonably small compass. Out of the vast multitude of saints he chose especially those who were honoured in Italy. His labours were lightened by some use of the " Mirror of History," the third part of a voluminons " Speculum Mundi," composed by Vincent de Beauvais, tutor to the sons of Louis IX.

One cannot but admit that some of Jacobus de Voragine's originals have suffered loss by the process to which they were subjected. Still the Golden Legend makes its claim on our attention as the favourite manual of the most popular literature of the middle ages. Although its comparatively small size was the cause no doubt of the very large measure of acceptance which the book received, we should hardly describe it as short, at least from a modern point of view. The earliest printed Latin copy in the British Museum (Basle 1474) is a substantial folio containing 244 chapters including 26 notices of Festivals and Fasts. In the hands of numerous editors and translators, who felt themselves at liberty to make additions as they pleased, the bulk of the volume was almost doubled. Caxton's edition with its 448 chapters is the largest, but the French version which he followed (Paris, 1480) is not far off with 440.

Among the varied contents of this storehouse of medieval lore there was much which might very probably not be unfitted to serve its original purpose of edification for the readers of any age. But we are not concerned here with the thirteenth century theology and ethics expounded by the Dominican preacher. Other hands before ours doubtless have turned over these pages and rested only at a tale. The Golden Legend is a story-book : and few stories have exercised greater fascination than some which appear among the lives of the saints. The regard due to the "forcible witnesses of ancient truth, provocations to the exercise of all piety," as Hooker calls them, who are unquestionably to be found in the church's roll of honour need not be lessened when we recognize that fancy has been largely at work within the limits of the calendar. "Legends in which noble men and women, Saints and Holy Virgins, were at issue with power, with cruelty, with fate" (Milman), formed not only lections devoutly listened to in church, but were also the recreations of castle, monastery or hut. A queen would ask a troubadour to sing the "lay of Brendan" or the tale of mild Margaret and her triumph over the "loathly worm" would uplift the heart of another "full fair maiden her flocks keeping," the peasant girl of France, Joan of Arc. The legends took shape in countless manners; sometimes the impression created by an attractive character was embodied in a tale; in not a few instances so thick a network of fiction has been woven round some venerated name that, like the ivy which clings round an ancient tree, it goes near to hide from all recognition the support on which it grew. Sometimes the passion for creating fresh objects of reverence found evidence for the existence of saints where a colder inspection has been unable to discover it. Sometimes the agent at work has been the grotesque humour which relieved with lighter touches the grim combat of the saints with ever-present forces of evil. In this channel too flowed stores of the imagination accumulated elsewhere : old materials drawn from quite other regions were used afresh in the legendary. Folklore contributed its share as in the stories of Saint Barlaam and Saint Josaphat, Saint Julian Hospitator, and Saint Eustace; which take us to the familiar ground where the sons of kings are shut up in towers to escape inevitable perils, where wild animals talk and prophesy and where those whom the hero succours reappear in their true form bringing gifts and blessings. Recollections of heathen deities were remoulded into Christian shapes as probably in the case of Saint Ursula and of Saint Margaret;

solar myth ends its various career as the combat
of Saint George and the Dragon ; chivalric romance presented the calendar elsewhere with
Saint Roland and Saint Oliver,* and has supplied in the Golden Legend a setting for the
story of Saint Alban.   The extracts given in this
volume are intended principally to illustrate the
fanciful aspect of saintly literature.   "The
Legends," says Renan, "are not for the most part
historical, and yet they are marvellously instruc-
tive as regards the colour of the period to which
they belong and its manners."   Sometimes too
they have another interest in the fact that they
have furnished materials for art and literature.
As regards the latter, one need not point out the
particular instances in which Dante, Cervantes
and Shakespeare have found suggestions in that
field as represented here.

An enormous number of existing manuscripts
attests the popularity of the Golden Legend.
Those who desired to meet with it in their
native tongue were soon gratified by the appearance of Italian, German, French and Spanish
translations.   Early in the fourteenth century,
Jehan Belet produced a French rendering soon
followed by another the work of Jehan de Vignay,
who dedicated his labours to the wife of Philippe
de Valois, "Jeanne de Bourgogne par la grace de
Dieu royne de France."   The first English translation was "drawen out of Frensshe into Englisshe,

---

* Martiloge of Salisbury.   June 16th.   (p. 95.   Ed., Procter, London,
1893).

the yere of Our Lorde MCCCC. and XXXVIII."
by "frere John of Benynguay" (? Bungay).

Probably the size of the Golden Legend made
it's production seem rather too heavy an undertaking in the earliest years of the printing press.
But no book was more frequently reprinted between the years 1470-1520: one bibliographer
has reckoned as many as seventy-four editions up
to the end of the fifteenth century. The French
translation which issued from Lyons, in 1476, is
the first book printed in France with a date.
After the "red pale" had been set up for about
seven years in the Almonry at Westminster,
Caxton accomplished his edition, certainly the
most extensive of all his works. At one time he
was inclined to relinquish the task; "For as moche
as this werke was grete and over chargeable to me
taccomplisshe I feryd me in the begynnyng of
the translacion to have continued it, by cause of
the longe tyme of the translacion, and also in
thenpryntyng of ye same, and in maner halfe
desperate to have accomplissd it, was in purpose
to have lefte it." Fortunately a promise from
the Earl of Arundel to take a reasonable quantity
and to allow him a buck in summer and a doe in
winter encouraged him to persevere. In 1483,
therefore, appeared a heavy folio without titlepage
but with it's conclusion as follows:

"Thus endeth the legende named in latyn
legenda aurea, that is to say in englysshe the
golden legende. For lyke as golde passeth in
valewe alle other metalles, so thys legende ex-

cedeth alle other bookes, wherin ben conteyned
alle the hygh and grete festys of our lord, the
festys of our blessyd lady, the lyves, passyons and
myracles of many other sayntes, and other hystoryes and actes, as al allonge here afore is made
mencyon. Whiche werke I have accomplisshed
at the commaundemente and requeste of the noble
and puyssaunte erle and my special good lord
Wyllyam erle of arondel, and have fynysshed it
at Westmestre the twenty day of Novembre, the
yere of our lord MCCCCLXXXIII, and the
fyrst yere of the reygne of Kyng Rychard the
thyrd. By me Wyllyam Caxton."

A number of Old Testament stories were
added in this edition and also several lives of
English Saints who were represented in the
original only by Saint Thomas of Canterbury
and Saint Oswald. The compiling was done by
Caxton himself. " For as mocke as I had by me
a legende in frensshe and another in latyn, and the
thyrd in englysshe, whyche varyed in many and
dyvers places, and also many hystoryes were com-
prysed in ye two other bookes which were not
in the englysshe boke, and therfore I have
wryton one oute of ye sayd thre bookes, whyche
I have ordryd other wyse than ye sayd englysshe
legende is which was tofore made." The
" englysshe legende " provided him with the life
of Saint Alban, and most of the lives of English
Saints are to be found in manuscript elsewhere.

A slightly altered second edition is dated at .
1487. Caxton had a third in hand at the time of

his death in 1491, which was produced two years afterwards by his successor Wynkyn de Worde. Fifteen copies of the Legend were " bequothen " in his will to Saint Margaret's, Westminster : the parish accounts shew that fourteen were sold and one retained apparently for use in the church.

Wynkyn de Worde multiplied copies in three editions up to 1527. But the Reformation was at hand and the Golden Legend was little fitted to face unprosperous weather. It has been pointed out as a curious coincidence that while Wynkyn de Worde was putting into type the last edition of the Golden Legend, William Tyndale was printing the New Testament in Cologne. Every English copy of the book bears traces of the change : for the life of Saint Thomas of Canter-bury, a special object of Henry VIII's aversion is always carefully scored out. In the controversies of the sixteenth century the Golden Legend was discredited on all sides alike by those who re-garded its legendary contents as ensnaring deceits and by those who objected to burden their cause by defence of its obvious unveracity. As early as 1543, Claude d'Espence, rector of the University of Paris, dared to describe it from the pulpit as " Legenda ferrea," but the sentiment met with so little approval that he was forced to make a pub-lic recantation. Bacon, however, was exposed to no such danger when he treated the book as an example of lying in his Essay on Atheism, " I had rather believe all the fables in the Legend, and the Talmud, and the Alcoran, than that this universal frame is without a mind." The judgment of the seventeenth century is summed up there and in the vigorous denunciation of Edward Leigh of Magdalen Hall, Oxford. "A book written by a man of a leaden heart for the baseness of the errours that are without wit or reason and of a brasen forehead for his impudent boldnesse in reporting things so fabulous and incredible." (A treatise of Religion and Learning, 1656, p. 242.)

One can scarcely think that the old hagiographer, who merely told the facts as he supposed he found them, deserved such hard measure. Modern readers could probably find books more efficacious to "encreace in them virtue and expelle vyce and synne." However, as the preface to the Morte d'Arthur says, "For to passe the tyme thys book shal be pleasaunt to rede in, but for to gyve fayth and byleve that al is trewe that is conteyned herin, ye be at your lyberte."

The text of these extracts is on the whole that of Caxton, but I have not hesitated to follow Wynkyn de Worde (1527) where he seemed to give a smoother reading, and to make such alterations or omissions as seemed likely to render the book "pleasannt to rede in." The Kelmscott Press edition (1892) has given me much help. I hope that I am not wrong in believing that most readers prefer a modernized spelling. A few notes are added, but little is said about those lives which are dealt with in such easily accessible

sources of information as Baring Gould's "Lives
of the Saints" and "Curious Myths of the Middle
Ages," Alban Butler's "Lives of the Saints," and
Mrs. Jameson's "Sacred and Legendary Art."

CONTENTS.

I.—AT THE NATIVITY OF OUR LORD.

HEN the world had endured five thousand and nine hundred years, Octavius the Emperor commanded that all the world should be inscribed, so that he might know how many cities, how many towns, and how many persons he had in all the universal world. Then was so great peace in the earth that all the world was obeisant to him. And, therefore, Our Lord would be born in that time that it should be known that he brought peace from heaven. And this Emperor commanded that every man should go into the towns, cities, or villages from whence they were of, and should bring with them a penny in knowledging that he was subject to the Empire of Rome. And by so many pence as should be found received should be known the number of the persons. Joseph which then was of the lineage of David, and dwelled in Nazareth, went into the city of Bethlehem, and led with him the Virgin Mary his wife. And when they were come thither, by cause the hostelries were all taken up, they were constrained to be without in a common place where all people went. And there was a stable for an ass that he brought with him, and for an

ox.   In that night our Blessed Lady and Mother
of God was delivered of Our Blessed Saviour
upon the hay that lay in the rack.

At which Nativity our Lord shewed many
miracles.   For because that the world was in so
great peace the Romans had done make a temple
which was named the Temple of Peace.   On
which they counselled with Apollo to know how
long it should stand and endure.   Apollo answered
to them that it should stand as long till a maid
had brought forth and borne a child.   And,
therefore, they did do write on the portal of the
temple, "Lo, this is the Temple of Peace that
ever shall endure."   For they supposed well that
a maid might never bear nor bring forth a child.
This temple the same time that Our Lady was
delivered and Our Lord born, overthrew and fell
down.   Of which Christian men afterward made
in the same place a church of Our Lady, which
is called Sancta Maria rotunda, that is to say,
the Church of Saint Mary the round.

Also the same night, as recordeth Innocent the
Third which was pope, there sprang and sourded
in Rome the same night a well or fountain that
ran largely all the night and all that day unto the
river called Tiber.

Also after that recordeth Saint John Chrysostom,
the III kings were this night in their orisons and
prayers upon a mountain when a star appeared to
them, which had the form of a right fair child
that had a cross in his forehead, which said to
these three kings that they should go to Jerusalem,

and there they should find the son of a virgin, God and man, which then was born.

Also there appeared in the orient three suns, which little and little assembled together, and were all in one: as it is signified to us that these three things be the Godhead, the soul, and the body, which be in three natures assembled in one person.

Also, Octavius the Emperor, like as Innocent recordeth, was much desired of his council and of his people that he should do men worship him as God, for never had there been tofore him so great a master and lord of the world as he was. Then the Emperor sent for a prophetess named Sybil for to demand of her if there were any so great and like him in the earth, or if any should come after him. Thus at the hour of mid-day she beheld the heaven and saw a circle of gold about the sun, and in the middle of the circle a maid holding a child in her arms. Then she called the Emperor and shewed it to him. When Octavius saw that he marvelled over much. Whereof Sybil said to him: "Hic puer major te est, ipsum adora." "This child is a greater lord than thou art, worship him." Then when the Emperor understood that this child was a greater lord than he was, he would not be worshipped as God, but worshipped this child that should be born. Wherefore the Christian men made a church of the chamber of the Emperor and named it Ara Cæli.

AGNES is said of agna, a lamb, for she was humble and debonair as a lamb, or of agno in Greek, which is to say, debonair and piteous, for she was debonair and merciful. Or Agnes of agnoscendo, for she knew the way of truth. And after this Saint Austin saith, truth is opposed against vanity, falseness, and doubleness, for these three things were taken from her for the truth that she had.

The blessed virgin Saint Agnes was much wise and well taught as Saint Ambrose witnesseth that wrote her passion. She was fair of visage but much fairer in the Christian faith. She was young of age and aged in wit. For in the xiiith year of her age she lost the death that the world giveth and found life in Jesus Christ, which when she came from school the son of the prefect of Rome for the Emperor loved her. And when his father and mother knew it, they offered to give much riches with him if he might have her in marriage, and offered to Saint Agnes precious gems and jewels, which she refused to take. Whereof it happed that the young man was ardently esprised in the love of Saint Agnes and came again and took with him more precious and richer adornments made with all manner of precious stones and, as well by his parents as by himself, offered to Saint Agnes rich gifts and possessions and all the delights and pleasures of the world and all to the end to have her in marriage.

But Saint Agnes answered to him in this manner: "Go from me, thou fardel of sin, nourishing of evils and morsel of death and depart. Know thou that I am prevented, and am loved of another lover which hath given to me many better jewels, which hath fianced me by his faith and is much more noble of lineage than thou art and of estate. He hath clad me with precious stones and with jewels of gold. He hath set in my visage a sign that I receive none other spouse but Him, and hath shewed me over great treasures which he must give me if I abide with Him. I will have none other spouse but him, I will seek none other. In no manner may I leave him. With Him am I firm and fastened in love which is more noble, more puissant and fairer than any other, whose love is much sweet and gracious, of whom the chamber is now ready for to receive me, where the virgins sing merrily. I am now embraced of Him of whom the mother is a virgin, and His Father knew never woman. To whom the angels serve. The sun and the moon marvel them of His beauty. Whose works never fail, whose riches never minish, by whose odour dead men rise again to life, by whose touching the sick men be comforted, whose love is chastity.

To Him I have given my faith, to Him I have commended my heart. When I love Him then am I chaste and when I touch Him then am I pure and clean, and when I take Him then am I a virgin. This is the love of my God."

When the young man had heard all this, he was despaired as he that was taken in blind love and was over sore tormented in so much that he lay down sick on his bed for the great sorrow that he had. Then came the physicians and anon knew his malady and said to his father that he languished of love that he had to some woman. Then the father enquired and knew that it was this woman, and did do speak to Saint Agnes for his son and said to her how his son languished for her love. Saint Agnes answered that in no wise she would break the faith of her first husband. Upon that the provost demanded who was her first husband of whom she so much vaunted and in his power so much trusted. Then one of her servants said that she was Christian and that she was so enchanted that she said Jesus Christ was her spouse. And when the provost heard that she was Christian he was full glad because to have power on her: for then the Christian people were in the will of the lord that if they would not deny their God or their belief all their goods should be forfeited.

Wherefore then the provost made Saint Agnes to come in justice and he examined her sweetly: and after cruelly by menaces. Saint Agnes well comforted said to him: "Do what thou wilt, for

my purpose shalt thou never change." And when
she saw him now flattering and now terrible
angry, she scorned him. And the provost said
to her being all angry : " One of two things thou
shalt choose: Either do sacrifice to our gods
with the virgins of the goddess Vesta, or go to
the brothel to be abandoned to all that thither
come to the great shame and blame of all thy
lineage." Saint Agnes answered: " If thou
knewest who is my God, thou wouldest not say
to me such words. But forasmuch as I know
the virtue of my God, I set no thing by thy
menaces. For I have His angel which is keeper
of my body." And thus Saint Agnes, that refused to do sacrifice to the idols, was delivered
naked to go to the brothel.

But anon as she was unclothed, God gave to
her such grace that the hairs of her head became
so long that they covered her to her feet so that
her body was not seen. And when Saint Agnes
entered, anon she found the angel of God ready
to defend her and environed Saint Agnes with a
bright clearness in such wise that no man might
see her nor come to her: There made she her
oratory and in making her prayers unto God, she
saw before her a white vesture and anon therewith she clad her and said: " I thank thee, Jesus
Christ, which accountest me with thy virgins and
hast sent me this vesture." All they that entered
made honour and reverence to the great clearness
that they saw about Saint Agnes and came out
more devout and more clean than they entered.

At the last came the son of the provost with a
great company for to accomplish his foul desires
and lusts. And when he saw his fellows come
out and issue all abashed, he mocked them and
called them cowards. And then he all enraged
entered for to accomplish his evil will. And
when he came to the clearness, he advanced him
to take the virgin : and anon the devil took him
by the throat and strangled him that he fell down
dead.

And when the provost heard these tidings of
his son, he ran weeping to the place and began,
crying, to say to Saint Agnes : "Oh thou cruel
woman, why hast thou shewed thy enchantment
on my son ?" and demanded her how his son was
dead and by what cause. To whom Saint Agnes
answered, "He took him into his power to whom
he had abandoned his will." "Why be not all
they dead," said he "that entered here to fore
him ?" "For his fellows saw the miracle of
the great clearness and were afeard and went
their way unhurt, for they did honour to my
God which hath clad me with this vestment and
hath kept my body. But your villainous son
as soon as he entered this house began to bray
and cry, and, when he would have laid hand upon
me, anon the devil slew him as thou seest." "If
thou mayst raise him," said he, "it may well appear that thou hast not put him to death." And
Saint Agnes answered, "Go ye all out that I may
make my prayer to God." And when she was
in her prayers, the angel came and raised him to

life. And anon he went out and began to cry with a high voice that the God of Christian men was very God in heaven, and in earth, and in the sea, and that the idols were vain that they worshipped, which might not help themself ne none other.

Then the bishops of the idols made a great discord among the people, so that all they cried, "Take away this sorceress and witch that turneth men's minds and alieneth their wits." When the provost saw these marvels, he would gladly have delivered Saint Agnes because she had raised his son: but he doubted to be banished. And he set in his place a lieutenant named Aspasius for to satisfy the people. And because he could not deliver her he departed sorrowfully.

Then Aspasius did do make a great fire among all the people and did do cast Saint Agnes therein. Anon as this was done, the flame departed into two parts, and burnt them that made the discords: and she abode all whole without feeling the fire. The people weened that she had done all by enchantment. Then made Saint Agnes her orison unto God thanking Him that she was escaped from the peril to lose her virginity and also from the burning of the flame. And when she had made her orison the fire lost all its heat and quenched. Aspasius, for the doubtance of the people, commanded to put a sword in her body: and so she was martyred.

Anon came the Christian men and the parents of Saint Agnes and buried her body. But the heathen defended it, and so cast stones at them that unneth* they escaped. She suffered martyrdom in the time of Constantine the Great, which began to reign the year of our Lord CCCIX.

Among them that buried her body there was one Emerentiana which had been fellow unto Saint Agnes howbeit she was not yet Christened but a holy virgin. She came also to the sepulchre of Saint Agnes, which constantly reproved the Gentiles and of them she was stoned and slain. Anon there came an earth quave, lightning and thunder that many of the paynims perished so that forthon the Christian people might surely come to the sepulcure unhurt.

It happed that when the friends of Saint Agnes watched at her sepulchre on a night, they saw come a great multitude of virgins all clad in vestments of gold and silver and a great light shone tofore them. And on the right side was a lamb more whiter than snow. And they saw also Saint Agnes among the virgins, which said to her parents, "Take heed and see that ye bewail me no more as dead but be ye joyful with me. For with all these virgins Jesus Christ hath given me most brightest habitation and dwelling. And I am with Him joined in heaven whom in earth I loved with my thought."

And this was the viiith day after her passion. And because of this vision holy church maketh memory of her the eighth day of the feast after which is called Agnetis Secundo.

* Scarcely.

III.—THE LEGEND OF SAINT ALBAN.

FTER that Julius Cæsar, the first Emperor of Rome, had divided the land of France, he made a shipping into Great Britain, which now is called England, in the time of Cassibelan, King of the Britons. And twice he was driven out and the third time, by the help of one Androgeus, Duke of Kent, he had victory and conquered the realm and subdued it to Rome, and made it to pay yearly tribute. And he ordained and established certain statutes in this land which were long observed and kept. Among which, he ordained that none of this land should receive the order of knighthood but only at Rome by the hands of the Emperor: lest peradventure the rude people and unworthy should take upon them that order unworthily, which is of great dignity: and also they should make an oath never to rebel nor bear arms against the Emperor: which statutes were used in all places obedient to Rome and under their subjection.

Then reigned in the land of Britain which now is called England a King named Severus, which for to please the Emperor Diocletian sent his son that hight Bassian with many other lords' sons of Cornwall, Wales, Scotland and Ireland unto the number of a thousand five hundred and

forty.   Among which was a prince's son of
Wales in great array, which hight Amphibalus
a goodly young man and well learned in Latin,
French, Greek and Hebrew.   And there was in
his fellowship a lord's son of the city of Verulam
named Alban which was a well-disposed and
seemly young man and discreet in his governance.

And all this fellowship came prosperously to
Rome in the time when Zephyrus was pope of
Rome: which saw the great beauty of this young
company and had compassion that they were not
Christian, and laboured as much as he might to
convert them to the faith of Jesus Christ.   Among
all other he converted the prince's son of Wales,
Amphibalus and baptized him and informed him
secretly in the faith.   And this holy Amphibalus
forsook the pomp and glory of the world and took
on him wilful poverty for the love of Jesus
Christ and ever after continued his life in per-
fection.   Also there were many other converted
at that time whom Diocletian did seek but none
could he find.

Then he ordained a day in which these young
men should receive the order of knighthood of
the Emperor's hand : and he himself girded their
swords about them and informed them the rule
and estate of the order.   And when all the cere-
monies were done longing to the order, and the
oath sworn, Bassian, son of King Severus, desired
of the Emperor that he might prove the facts of
knighthood there in jousting and tourneying ;
which was granted to him and greatly allowed for

his manly desire and noble request. In which tourney and joust, Bassian and his fellowship had the prize and victory. And among all other, Alban was the best knight and most best proved in strength, wherefore he had a sovereign name to fore all other. Whose arms was of azure with a saltire of gold : which arms afterwards bore the noble king Offa first founder of the monastery called Saint Albans and he, bearing these arms, had ever glorious victory. And after his death he left those arms in the monastery of Saint Albans.

Then when Bassian and his fellowship had long sojourned in Rome, they asked licence of the Emperor to return home into Britain, which the Emperor granted to them all save to Alban ; whom for his manliness and his prowess he would retain to be in his service about his person. And so he abode with him there seven years. And after, for divers causes, Maximian, which was fellow to Diocletian, was sent in to Britain with a great army for to subdue the rebels. With whom Alban came and was ordained prince of his knights and so entered into Britain again.

In that time Saint Pontian sat in the see at Rome, which by himself and virtuous men that preached, and by shewing of miracles, converted unto the faith of Jesus Christ and christened in the city of Rome, lxvim men. And when the Emperor heard hereof, he assembled all the senators and kings, princes and lords, of every land being under the obedience of Rome, to have ad-

vice how he might destroy the Christian faith.
And then it was concluded that the Pope should
be damned with all his Christian people and be
punished with divers torments, and that all the
books of Christ's law should be burnt and churches
thrown down, and all men of holy church to be
slain in every place. Which ordinance, when it
was known among the Christian people of Rome
of divers parts of the world, then they went and
departed into their own country.

Among whom Saint Amphibalus, which long
had dwelled at Rome, departed and came home
into Britain again where he was born. And so
came unto Verulam; whereas none would receive
him into his house. And he walked about in the
streets abiding the comfort of God. And then it
happed he met with Alban which was lord of the
city and prince of the knights and steward of the
land, having about him a great multitude of servants, and at that time, Alban was richly arrayed
with clothes fringed with gold, to whom all the
people did great worship. Then Amphibalus
which had left the arms of a knight and was
arrayed like a clerk, knew well Alban but Alban
knew not him, how be it they had been tofore
both in one fellowship. And he desired and
prayed Alban of lodging for the love of God.
Alban without feigning, as he that alway loved to
do hospitality, granted him lodging and well
received him, and gave him meat and drink
necessary for him.

And after, when his servants were departed, he

went secretly to this pilgrim and said to him in this wise : "How is it," said he, "that thou art a Christian man and comest into these parts unhurt by the Gentiles?" To whom Saint Amphibalus said : "My Lord Jesus Christ, the Son of the living God, hath surely conducted me and hath kept me by His power from all perils. And the same Lord hath sent me into this land to preach and denounce to the people the faith of Jesus Christ, to the end that they should be made people acceptable to Him." To whom Alban said : "What is he that is the Son of God whom ye affirm to be Jesus Christ and son of the Virgin? These be new things to me for I have not heard of them. I would fain know what Christian men feel thereof." Then Amphibalus expounded to him and declared our faith and belief, in which anon Alban disputed again and said that by reason it might not be, and so departed from him.

And the next night after, Saint Alban saw in his dream all the mystery of our faith, as well how the Second Person of the Trinity came down and took our nature and became man and suffered death, and of His Resurrection and Ascension. Whereof he was greatly troubled and came on the morrow to Amphibalus and told him what he had dreamed. And then Saint Amphibalus thanked Our Lord and so informed him in the faith that Saint Alban was stedfast in the belief of Jesus Christ. And thus he kept his master Amphibalus in his house six weeks and more and always in a lodge apart they held their holy conversation, so long till at last they were espied and complained on unto the judge. Wherefore the judge sent for Alban and for the clerk.

And because that Amphibalus should go into Wales, Saint Alban did do clothe him like a knight and led him out·of the town, and departed with many tears, and they commended each other to the Lord. And after Saint Alban was sent for: which came, having on him the clerk's array and clothing, bearing a cross and an image of Our Lord hanging thereon, to the end that they should know verily that he was a Christian man. And the men that came for him drew him cruelly to the judge Asclepiodotus. And when the Paynims saw him bear the sign of the cross which was unknown to them, they were sore troubled and afeard.

Then the cruel judge demanded him whose servant he had been, and of what kindred, and because he would not tell, he was much wroth; but among many questions, he told him that his name was Alban and that he was a very Christian man. Then the judge demanded him where the clerk was that entered into the city now late, speaking of Christ. "He is come for to beguile and deceive our citizens, know ye well he would have come into our presence but that his conscience hath removed him; and he hath mistrust in his cause, and guile and falseness is hid under his doctrine. Thou mayest well know, and evidently understand, that thou hast given thy consent to a foolish man. Wherefore, forsake his doctrine

and repent thee and make satisfaction for thy
trespass in doing sacrifice to our Gods. And that
done, thou shalt not only have forgiveness of thy
sin, but thou shalt have towns and provinces,
men, gold and power." Then said Alban to the
judge: "O thou judge, the words and menaces
that thou hast spoken be but vain and superfluous.
It is openly known that this clerk, if it had
thought him good and profitable, and also if our
both hearts had accorded thereto, he had come to
thine audience. But I would not assent thereto
knowing that this people is ever ready to do evil.
I knowledge that I have received his doctrine
and repent me nothing thereof. For the faith
that I have received restoreth the feeble and sick
to their health, for the deed proveth it. This
faith is more dear to me than all the riches that
thou promisest me, and more precious than all
the worship that thou purposest to give me. For
shortly your gods be false and failing: for they
that most busily serve them be most wretchedly
deceived."

Then came anon forth a great multitude of
Paynims, and with force and strength would compel him to do sacrifice, and commanded him to
offer to the gods: but in no wise would he consent to their cursed rites. And by the commandment of the judge, he was taken and stretched
abroad to be scourged. And as he was grievously
beaten, he turned him to Our Lord with a glad
visage and said: "My Lord Jesus Christ, I
beseech Thee keep my mind that it move not

B

nor that it fall from the estate that Thou hast set
it in. For, Lord, with all my heart I offer my
soul to Thee in very sacrifice, and I desire to be
made Thy witness by shedding of my blood."
These words sounded he among his beatings, and
the tormentors beat him so long that their hands
waxed weary and the people hoped that Saint
Alban would change his purpose. And therefore
he was kept under the governance of the judge
six weeks and more. And all that time the
elements bare witness of the injury done to holy
Alban. For, from the time of his taking to the
time that he was delivered from the bands of his
flesh, there came never dew nor rain upon the
earth, but burning heat of the sun, and also in the
nights, all that time was unsufferable heat: so
that neither trees nor fields brought forth no
fruit. And thus the elements fought for this
holy man against the wicked men.

And the judge Asclepiodotus dreaded for to
slay him, by cause of the great love that the
Emperor had to him, and for reverence of his
dignity and power of his kindred, unto the time
that he had informed Diocletian of his conversation. And when the Emperor had seen the
letters, anon Maximian came into Britain for to
destroy the faith of Jesus Christ. And he was
commanded that no Christian men should be
spared save only Alban; whom they should entreat,
to pervert him by fair promises and fear him by
menaces, and so to compel him to turn again to
to their sect. And if he would in no wise leave

the Christian faith, then he to have capital sentence and be beheaded by some knight, for the worship of the order of knighthood. And the clerk that converted him to suffer the foulest death that could be imagined, that the beholders thereof may have dread and horror of semblable pains.

And when Maximian came into Britain, he took with him the king Asclepiodotus, and went straight to the city of Verulam for to fulfil the commandment of the Emperor. And then Saint Alban was brought forth tofore them out of prison, and by all the ways that they could imagine they attempted to pervert him ; but the holy man was constant and firm in the faith. Whereof they having indignation, ordained a day of justice, which day come, they gave sentence on Saint Alban that he should be beheaded ; which sentence was given under writing.

Then all the burgesses of Verulam, of London, and other towns about, were summoned to come the next Thursday following for to hear the judgment, and see the execution upon Alban, prince of knights, and steward of Britain. At which day came people without number for to see this said execution. And then was Alban brought out of prison whom they desired to make sacrifice to Jupiter and Appollyn : which utterly refused it but preached the faith of Christ, that he converted much people to be christened.

Then Maximian and Asclepiodotus gave final sentence on him, thus saying : " In the time of the Emperor Diocletian, Alban, lord of Verulam, prince of knights, and steward of all Britain, during his life, hath despised Jupiter and Appollyn our Gods, and to them hath done derogation and disworship. Wherefore by the law, he is judged to be dead by the hand of some knight: and the body to be buried in the same place where his head shall be smitten off: and his sepulchre to be made worshipfully for the honour of knighthood whereof he was prince. And also the cross that he bare and the pilgrim's cloak that he wore should be buried with him and his body to be closed in a chest of lead and so laid in his sepulchre. This sentence hath the law ordained because he hath renied our principal gods."

Then arose a great murmur among the people, and they said that they ought not to suffer such injury done to so noble and so good a man: and specially his kindred and friends which laboured full sore for his deliverance. Whereof Alban was afeard to be delivered from his passion at their request and instance, and stood up holding the cross, looking toward heaven and saying, "Lord God Jesus Christ, I beseech thee that thou suffer not the fiend to prevail against me by his deceits and that the people let not my martyrdom." And then he turned to the people, saying, "Wherefore tarry ye and lose the time and why execute not ye on me the sentence? For I let you wit I am a great enemy to your gods, which have no power ne may do no thing, nor hear, nor see, nor understand, to whom none of you would be like. O what vanity and what blindness is among you to worship such idols, and will not know Jesus Christ the only son of God, and His very true law."

Then the paynims spake together and assented that he should be put to death. And they chose a place where he should be executed named Holmeshurst. But then arose a contention among the people what death he should suffer: some would have him crucified like as Christ was, other would have him buried quick. But the judge and the people of the city would have him beheaded according to the commandment of the Emperor.

And so he was led forth towards his martyrdom; and all the people to the place following this holy man with despiteous words and rebukes. Whereto this blessed man Alban answered no word but meekly and patiently suffered all their reproofs. And the people were so great a multitude that they occupied all the place which was large and great; and the heat of the sun was so great that it burnt and scalded their feet as they went.

And so they led him till they came to a swift running river where they might not lightly pass for the press of the people. For many were shift over the bridge into the water and were drowned: and many because they might not go over the bridge for press, unclothed them for to swim over the river: and some that could not

swim presumed to do the same and were wretchedly drowned, ·whereof was a great rumour and
noise piteously among the people.

And when Saint Alban perceived this thing,
he wailed and wept for the harm and death of
his enemies that so were perished : and kneeled
down, holding his hand up to God, beseeching
Him that the water might be lessed and the flood
withdrawn, that the people might be near him at
his passion.   And forthwith God shewed at the
request of Saint Alban a fair miracle.   For the
water withdrew and the river dried up in such
wise that the people might safely go dry foot
over the river.   And also by the prayer of this
holy man they that tofore had been drowned
were restored again to life and were founden
alive in the deepness of the river.

And then one of the knights that drew Saint
Alban to his martyrdom saw these miracles that
God shewed for him and anon threw away his
sword and knelt down at the feet of Saint Alban,
saying: "I knowledge to God mine error and demand forgiveness," and wept sore and said : "O
Alban, servant of God, verily thy God is Almighty
and there is no God but He.   And therefore I
knowledge me to be His servant during my life :
for this river by thy prayers is made dry.   Wherefore I bear witness that there is no god but thy
God which doeth such miracles."   And when he
had said thus their fury and woodness increased
and they said unto him: "Thou art false: for it
is not as thou sayest, ne as thou affirmest, for

this river is thus dried up by the benignity of our gods. And therefore we worship Jupiter and Appollyn which for our ease hath taken up this water by the great heat. And because thou takest away the worship of our gods, and rewardest it to other by evil interpretation, thou hast deserved the pain which longeth to a blasphemer." And then forthwith they drew out the teeth of his head: and the holy mouth that had borne witness of truth was grievously beaten with so many of them, that or they left they tare all the members of his body, and to brake all his bones, and all to rent his body and left him lying upon the sand.

But who might without weeping of tears express how this holy man Alban was drawn and led through briars and thorns and sharp stones, that the blood of his feet coloured the way as they went and the stones were bloody. Then at the last they came to a hill where this holy Alban should finish and end his life. In which place lay a great multitude of people nigh dead for heat of the sun and for thirst. When they saw Alban they grinted with their teeth upon him for anger, saying: "O thou most wicked man, how great is thy wickedness that makest us to die with thy sorcery and witchcraft in this great misery and heat." Then Alban having pity on them sorrowed by great affection for them and said: "Lord, that madest man's body of earth and his soul unto thy likeness, suffer not these creatures to perish for any cause committed

against me.   And blessed Lord, make the air at-
temperate and send them water to refresh them."
And then anon the wind blew a fresh cool, and
also at the feet of this holy man Alban sprang up
a fair well, whereof all the people marvelled to
see the cold water spring up in the hot sandy
ground and so high, on the top of an hill: which
water flowed all about and in large streams running down the hill.   And then the people ran
to the water and drank so that they were well
refreshed: and thus by the merits of Saint Alban
their thirst was clean quenched.

But yet for all the great goodness that was
shewed they thirsted strongly for the blood of
this holy man and bound him first to a stake, and
after hung him on a bough by the hair of his
head, and sought among the people one to smite
off his head. · And then a cruel man was ready
and in an anger took his sword and smote off the
head of this holy man at one stroke, that the
body fell to the ground and the head hung still
on the bough.   And the tormentor as he had
smitten off his head, both his eyes started out of
his head and the wretch might in no wise be
restored again to his sight.   Then many of the
paynims said that this vengeance came of great
rightwiseness.

Then the knight which was left for dead upon
the sand a little before, enforced himself as much
as he might and crept upon his hands unto the
top of the hill whereas Saint Alban was beheaded.
And the judge, seeing him, began to scorn him

and all the miracles that had been shewed by
Saint Alban. And he said to him: "O thou
lame and crooked, now pray to thine Alban that
he restore thee to thy first health. Run and hie
thee, and take the head, by which thou mayest
receive thine healing. Why tarriest thou so
long? Go and bury his body and do him service." Then this knight burning in charity,
said: "I believe firmly that the blessed Alban
by his merits may get to me perfect health,
and get to me of Our Lord that which ye say
in scorn." And when he had thus said he took
and embraced the holy head in his arms and
reverently loosed it from the bough and set it
fair to the body. And by the miracle of Our
Lord, he was forthwith restored to his first health
and forthwith began to preach the great power
of Our Lord Jesus Christ and of the great merits
of Saint Alban. And then he was stronger to
labour than ever he was before, whereof he gave
thankings and laud to God and to this holy martyr Saint Alban. And there in the same place,
he buried the holy body, and laid a fair tomb
over him. And afterward the paynims took this
knight and bound him to a stake, and after smote
off his head that same day. And after the judge
gave licence to the people to depart and go
home.

And the night after, was seen a fair beam
coming down from heaven to the sepulchre of
Saint Alban, by which angels descended and ascended all the night during, singing heavenly

songs, among which this song was heard : "Alban the glorious man is a noble martyr of Jesus Christ." And all the people came to behold this sight : wherefore many were turned from their false belief and believed in Jesus Christ.

IV.—THE LEGEND OF SAINT BARLAAM
AND SAINT JOSAPHAT.

BARLAAM is he of whom Saint John Damascene made the history with great diligence, in whom Divine grace so wrought that he converted to the faith Saint Josaphat. And then as all Ind was full of Christian people and of monks, there arose a puissant king which was named Avennir, which made great persecution to Christian men, and specially to monks.

And it happed so that one which was friend of the king and chief in his palace, by the inspiration of Divine grace, he left the hall royal for to enter into the order of monks. And when the king heard say that he was Christian he was wood for anger, and did do seek him through every desert till that he was found with great pain, and then he was brought tofore him. And when he saw him in a vile coat and much lean for hunger which was wont to be covered with precious clothing and abounded in much riches, he said to him, "O thou fool and out of thy mind, why hast thou changed thine honour into villainy, and art made the player of children ?"

And he said to him, "If thou hear of me reason, put from thee thine enemies." Then the king demanded him who were his enemies. And he said to him, "Ire and covetise, for they empeach and let that truth may not be seen, and to assay prudence and equity." To whom the king said, "Let it be as thou sayest." And that other said, "The fools despise the things that be, like as they were not: and he that hath not the taste of the things that be, he shall not use the sweetness of them and he may not learn the truth from the things that be not." And when he had shewed many things of the mystery of the Incarnation, the king said to him, "If I had not promised thee at the beginning that I should put away ire from my counsel, I should cast thy body into the fire. Go thy way and flee from my eyes that I see thee no more and that I distress thee not." Anon the man of God went his way all heavy because he had not suffered martyrdom.

Then in the meanwhile it happed to the king which had no child that there was a fair son born of his wife and he was called Josaphat. And then the king assembled a right fair company of people for to make sacrifice to his gods for the nativity of his son : and also assembled lv astronomers of whom he enquired what should befall his son. And they said to him that he should be great in power and in riches. And one more wise than another said, "Sir, this child that is born shall not be under thy reign, but he shall

be in another much better without comparison.
And know that I suppose that he shall be of
Christian religion, which thou persecutest." And
that said he not of himself but he said it by inspiration of God.

And when the king heard that, he doubted
much and did do make without the city a right
noble palace, and therein set he his son for to
dwell and abide. And set right fair younglings,
and commanded them that they should not speak
to him of death, nor of old age, nor of sickness,
nor of poverty, nor of no thing that may give
him cause of heaviness: "but say to him all
things that be joyous, so that his mind may be
esprized with gladness, and that he think on no
thing to come." And anon as any of his servants
were sick, the king commanded for to take him
away, and set another whole in his stead: and
commanded that no mention should be made to
him of Jesus Christ.

In that time was with the king a man which
was secretly Christian, and was chief among all
the noble princes of the king. And as he went
on a time to hunt with the king, he found a poor
man lying on the ground which was hurt on the
foot of a beast: which prayed that he would receive him and that he might of him be holpen by
some mean. And the knight said, "I shall receive
thee gladly, but I wot not how that thou mayest
do any profit." And he said to him, "I am a
leech of words, and if any be hurt by words I can
well give him a medicine." And the knight set

it at nought all that he said, but he received him
only for God's sake and healed him.   And then
some princes envious and malicious saw that this
prince was so great and gracious with the king,
and accused him to the king and said that he was
not only turned to the Christian faith, but enforced to withdraw from him his realm : and that
he moved and solicited the company and counselled them thereto.   "And if thou wilt know
it," said they, "then call him secretly and say to
him that this life is soon done, and therefore thou
wilt leave the glory of the world and of thy realm.
And affirm that thou wilt take the habit of monks,
whom thou hast so persecuted by ignorance, and
after thou shalt see what he shall answer."   And
when the king had done all that they had said,
the knight, that knew nothing of the treason,
began to weep, and praised much the counsel of
the king, and remembered him of the vanity of
the world and counselled him to do it as soon as
he might.   And when the king heard him say so,
he supposed it had been true that the other had
said to him : how be it he said no thing.   And
then the knight understood and apperceived that
the king had taken his words in evil, and went
and told all this unto the leech of words all by
order.   And he said to him, "Know thou for
truth, that the king feareth that thou wilt assail
his realm.   Arise thou to-morrow and shave off
thine hair and do off thy vestments, and clothe
thee in hair in manner of a monk, and go early
to the king.   When he shall demand thee what

thou meanest, thou shalt answer, "My lord the king, I am ready to follow thee : for if the way thou desirest to go be hard, if I be with thee, it shall be the lighter to thee : and like as thou hast had me in prosperity so shalt thou have me in adversity. I am all ready, wherefore tarriest thou ?" And when he had thus done and said by order, the king was abashed and reproved the false men and did him more honour than he did before.

And after this the king's son, that was nourished in the palace, came to age and grew and was plainly taught in all wisdom. And he marvelled wherefore his father had so enclosed him, and called one of his servants which was most familiar with him secretly, and demanded him of this thing: and said to him that he was in great heaviness that he might not go out, and that his meat nor drink savoured him not nor did him no good. And when his father heard this, he was full of sorrow. And anon he let do make ready horses and joyful fellowship to accompany him, in such wise that no thing dishonest should happen to him. And on a time thus as the king's son went he met a lazar and a blind man. And when he saw them he was abashed and enquired what them ailed, And his servants said, "These be passions that come to men" And he demanded if those passions came to all men. And they said, nay. Then said he, "Be they which shall suffer these passions known without fail ?" And they answered, "Who is he that may know the adventures of men ?" And he began to be much anguished for the incustomable thing hereof. And another time he found a man much aged which had his cheer wrinkled, his teeth fallen, and was all crooked for age. Whereof the king's son was abashed and said he desired to know the miracle of this vision. And when he knew that this was because he had lived many years, then he demanded to know what should be the end. And they said, death. And he said, "Is then the death the end of all men or of some ?" And they said for certain that all men must die. And when he knew that all should die, he demanded them in how many years that should happen. And they said in old age of fourscore years or an hundred, and after that age the death followeth. And this young man remembered oft in his heart these things and was in great discomfort. But he shewed him much glad tofore his father, and he desired much to be enformed and taught in these things.

And then there was a monk of perfect life and good opinion that dwelled in the desert of the land of Sennaar named Barlaam. And this monk knew by the Holy Ghost what was done about this king's son, and took the habit of a merchant, and came unto the city and spake to the greatest governor of the king's son. And he said to him, "I am a merchant and have a precious stone to sell which giveth sight to blind men, and hearing to deaf men. It maketh the

dumb to speak and giveth wisdom to fools. And
therefore bring me to the king's son and I shall
deliver it to him." To whom he said, "Thou
seemest a man of prudent nature, but thy words
accord not to wisdom. Nevertheless that I have
knowledge of that stone shew it me, and if it be
such as thou sayest, and so proved, thou shalt
have great honour of the king's son." To whom
Barlaam said, "My stone hath yet such virtue,
that he that seeth it and hath none whole sight
and keepeth not entire chastity, if he haply see it
the virtue of seeing that he hath, he should lose
it. And I that am a physician see well that thou
hast not thy sight whole; but I understand that
the king's son is chaste and hath right fair eyes
and whole." And then the man said, "If it be
so, shew it not to me, for mine eyes be not whole,
and I am foul of sin." And Barlaam said, "This
thing appertaineth to the king's son, and therefore bring me to him anon." And he anon told
this to the king's son and brought him in and he
received him honourably.

And then Barlaam said to him, "Thou hast
done well, for thou hast not taken heed of my
littleness that appeareth withoutforth. But thou
ast done like to a noble king which, when he
rode in his chair clad with clothes of gold and
met with poor men which were clad with torn
clothes, anon he sprang out of his chair and fell
down to their feet and worshipped them, and
after arose and kissed them. And his barons took
this evil and were afeard to reprove him thereof

But they said to his brother how the king had
done this thing against his royal majesty, and his
brother reproved him thereof. And the king had
such a custom that, when one should be delivered
to the death, the king should send his crier with
his trump that was ordained thereto. And on
the even he sent the crier with the trump before
his brother's gate, and made to sound the trump.
And when the king's brother heard this he was
in despair of saving of his life and could not
sleep all the night, and made his testament. And
on the morrow early he clad him in black, and
came weeping with his wife and children to the
king's palace. And the king made him come tofore him and said to him, 'A fool that thou art,
if thou hast heard the messenger of thy brother,
to whom thou knowest well thou hast not trespassed, and doubtest so much, how ought not I
then doubt the messengers of Our Lord against
whom I have so oft sinned? which signified unto
me more clearly the death than the trump and
shewed to me horrible coming of the judge'

And after this he did do make four chests and
did do cover two of them with gold withoutforth,
and did do fill them with bones of dead men and
filth : and the other two he did do pitch, and did
do fill them with precious stones and rich gems.
And after this the king did do call his great.
barons, because he knew well that they complained of him to his brother, and did do set these
four chests before them, and demanded of them
which were most precious. And they said that

the two that were gilt were most of value. Then
the king commanded that they should be opened
and anon a great stink issued out of them. And
the king said, 'These be like them that be
clothed with precious vestments and be full
withinforth of ordure and sin.' And after he
made open the others and there issued out a marvellous sweet odour. And the king said, 'These
be semblable to the poor men that I met and
honoured. For though they be clad in foul vestments, yet shine they withinforth with good
odour of good virtues. And ye take no heed but
to the withoutforth and consider not what is
within.' And thou hast done to me like as the
king did for thou hast well received me."

And after this Barlaam began to tell to him a
long sermon of the creation of the world, and of
the day of judgment, and of the reward of good
and evil, and began strongly to blame them that
worship idols. And told to him of their folly
such an example as followeth, saying, that an
archer took a little bird called a nightingale, and
when he would have slain this nightingale, there
was a voice given to this nightingale which said,
"O thou man what should it avail thee if thou
slay me? Thou mayest not fill thy belly with
me. But and if thou wilt let me go, I shall teach
thee three wisdoms, that, if thou keep them diligently, thou mayest have great profit thereof."
Then he was abashed of his words and promised
that he would let him go, if he would tell him
his wisdoms. Then the bird said to him, "Study

never to take that thing that thou mayest not take. And of things lost which may not be recovered, sorrow never therefore. Nor believe never thing that is incredible. Keep well these three things and thou shalt do well." And then he let the bird go as he had promised, and then the nightingale fleeing in the air said to him, "Alas, thou wretched man, thou hast had evil counsel, for thou hast lost this day great treasure. For I have in my bowels a precious margarite which is greater than the egg of an ostrich." And when he heard that he was much wroth and sorrowed sore because he had let her go, and enforced him all that he could to take her again, saying, "Come again to my house and I shall shew to thee all humanity and give to thee all that thou shalt need and after shall let thee go honourably whereas thou wilt." Then said the nightingale to him, "Now I know well that thou art a fool, for thou hast no profit in the wisdoms that I have said to thee. For thou art right sorrowful for me whom thou hast lost which am irrecuperable, and yet thou weenest to take me when thou mayest not come so high as I am. And furthermore thou believest to be in me a precious stone more than the egg of an ostrich when all my body may not attain to the greatness of such an egg." And in like wise be they fools that adore and trust in idols, for they worship that which they have made and call them whom they have made keepers of them.

And after he began to dispute against the fal-

lacies of the world and delight and vanity thereof,
and brought forth many examples and said :

"They that desire the delights corporal and
suffer their souls to die for hunger, be like to a
man that fled before an unicorn that he should
not devour him.   And in fleeing he fell into a
great pit.   And as he fell he caught a branch of a
tree with his hand and set his feet upon a sliding
place.   And then he saw two mice, that one
white and that other black, which without ceasing
gnawed the root of the tree, and had almost
gnawed it asunder.   And he saw in the bottom
of this pit an horrible dragon casting fire that had
his mouth open and desired to devour him. Upon
the sliding place on which his foot stood, he saw
the heads of four serpents which issued there.
And then he lifted up his eyes and saw a little
honey that hung on the boughs of the tree, and
forgot the peril that he was in and gave him all
to the sweetness of that little honey.   The unicorn is the figure of death, which continually followeth man and desireth to take him.   The pit is
the world which is full of all wickedness.   The
tree is the life of every man which by the two
mice, that be the day and the night and the hours
thereof, incessantly be wasted and approached to
the cutting or gnawing asunder. The place where
the four serpents were is the body ordained by
the four elements, by which the jointure of the
members is parted in bodies disordinate.   The
horrible dragon is the mouth of hell which desireth to devour all creatures.   The sweetness of the

honey on the boughs of the tree is the false deceivable delectation of the world by which man is deceived so that he taketh no heed of the peril that he is in."

And yet he said that they that love the world be semblable to a man that had three friends, of which he loved the first as much as himself, and he loved the second less than himself, and loved the third a little or nought. And it happed so that this man was in great peril of his life and was summoned before the king. Then he ran to his first friend and demanded of him his help, and told to him how he had always loved him. To whom the other said, " I have other friends with whom I must be this day, and I wot not who thou art, therefore I may not help thee. Yet nevertheless I shall give to thee two slops with which thou mayest cover thee." And then he went away much sorrowful and went to that other friend and required also his aid. And he said to him, " I may not attend to go with thee to this debate, for I have great charge. But I shall fellowship thee unto the gate of the palace, and then I shall return again and do mine own needs." And then he, being heavy and as despaired, went to the third friend and said to him, " I have no reason to speak to thee, for I have not loved thee as I ought; but I am in tribulation and without friends ; and I pray thee that thou wilt help me." And that other answered with glad cheer and said, "Certes, I confess to be thy dear friend, and have not forgotten the little benefit that thou hast done to me.

And I shall go right gladly with thee before the
king for to see what shall be demanded of thee,
and I shall pray the king for thee." The first
friend is possession of riches, for which man putteth him in many perils: and when the death
cometh he hath no more of it but a cloth for to
wind him in for to be buried. The second friend
is his sons, his wife and kin, which go with him
to his grave and anon return for to entend unto
their own needs. The third friend is faith, hope
and charity and other good works which we have
done : that when we issue out of our bodies they
may well go before us and pray God for us, and
they may well deliver us from the devils our enemies.

And yet he said according to this, that in a
certain city is a custom that they of the city
should choose every year a strange man and unknown to be their prince, and they shall give him
puissance to do whatsomever he will, and govern
the country without any other constitution. And
he being thus in great delights and weening ever
to continue, suddenly they of the city should
arise against him and lead him naked through the
city, and after send him in to an isle in exile, and
there he should find neither meat nor clothing,
but should be constrained to be perished for hunger and cold. And after that they would enhance
another to the kingdom : and thus they did long.
At the last they took one which knew their custom. And he sent before him into that isle great
treasure without number during all his year. And

when his year was accomplished and passed, he was put out and put to exile like the others. And whereas the others that had been before him perished from hunger and cold, he abounded in great riches and delights. And this city is the world, and the citizens be the princes of darkness which feed us with false delectation of the world, and then the death cometh when we take none heed and then we be sent in exile to the place of darkness. And the riches that be before sent be done by the hands of poor men.

And when Barlaam had perfectly taught the king's son, and he would leave his father for to follow him, Barlaam said to him, "If thou wilt do thus, thou wilt be semblable to a young man that, when he should have wedded a noble wife, forsook her and fled away and came in to a place where as he saw a virgin, daughter of an old poor man, that laboured and praised God with her mouth. To whom he said, 'What is this that thou doest, daughter, that art so poor and alway thou thankest God like as thou hadst received great things of Him?' To whom she said, 'Like as a little medicine oft delivereth a great langour and pain, right so for to give to God thankings alway of a little gift is made a giver of great gifts. For the things that be without forth be not ours, but they that be within us be ours. And therefore I have received great gifts of God, for He hath made me like to His image. He hath given to me understanding, He hath called me to His glory, and hath opened to me the gate of His

kingdom : and therefore for these gifts it is fitting
to me to give Him praising.' This young man
seeing her prudence, asked of her father to have
her to wife. To whom the father said, 'Thou
mayest not have my daughter, for thou art the son
of rich and noble kin, and I am but a poor man.'
But when he so sore desired her, the old man
said to him, 'I may not give her to thee, since
thou wilt lead her home in to the house of thy
father, for she is mine only daughter, and I have
no more.' And he said, 'I shall dwell with thee
and shall accord with thee in all things.' And
then he did off his precious vestments and did on
him the habit of the old man, and so dwelling with
him took her unto his wife. And when the old
man had long proved him, he led him in to his
chamber, and shewed to him great plenty of riches,
more than he ever had, and gave to him all."

And then Josaphat said to him. " This narra-
tion toucheth me convenably, and I trow thou
hast said this for me. Now say to me, father, how
many years art thou old and where conversest
thou, for from thee I will never depart." To
whom Barlaam said, "I have dwelled xlv years in
the desert of the land of Sennaar." To whom
Josaphat said, "Thou seemest better to be lxx
years." And he said, "If thou demandest of all
the years of my nativity thou hast well esteemed
them. But I account not in the number of my
life the years that I have dispended in the vanity
of the world. For I was then dead toward God,
and I number not the years of death with the

years of life." And when Josaphat would have followed him into desert, Barlaam said to him, "If thou do so I shall not have thy company, and I shall be then the author of persecution to my brethren. But when thou seest time convenable thou shalt come to me." And then Barlaam baptized the king's son and enformed him well in the faith and after returned in to his cell.

And a little while after the king heard say that his son was christened, wherefore he was much sorrowful. And one that was his friend, named Arachis, recomforting him said, "Sir king, I know right well an old hermit that resembleth much Barlaam, and he is of our sect. He shall feign him as he were Barlaam, and shall defend first the faith of Christian men and after shall leave and return from it, and thus your son shall return to you." And then the king went into desert as it were to fetch Barlaam and took this hermit and feigned that he had taken Barlaam. And when the king's son heard say that Barlaam was taken he wept bitterly. But afterward by revelation divine he knew that it was not he. Then the king went to his son and said to him, "Thou hast put me in great heaviness, thou hast dishonoured mine old age, thou hast darked the light of mine eyes, son, why hast thou done so? Thou hast forsaken the honour of my gods." He answered to him, "I have fled the darkness and am come to the light, I have fled error and know truth. And therefore thou travailest for nought for thou mayest never withdraw me from

Jesus Christ. For like as it is impossible to thee to touch the heaven with thy hand or for to dry the great sea, so is it to thee for to change me." Then the father said, "Who is cause hereof but I myself, who so gloriously have nourished thee, that never father nourished more his son? For which cause thine evil will hath made thee wood against me. And it is well right, for the astronomers in thy nativity said thou shouldest be proud and disobedient to thy parents. But and thou now wilt not obey me, thou shalt no more be my son, and I shalt be thine enemy for a father, and shall do to thee that I never did to mine enemies." To whom Josaphat said, " Father, wherefore art thou angry because I am made a partaker of good things? What father was ever sorrowful in the prosperity of his son? I shall no more call thee father but if thou be contrary to me I shall flee thee as a serpent."

Then the king departed from him in great anger and said to Arachis his friend all the hardness of his son. And he counselled the king that he should give him no sharp words, for a child is better reformed by fair and sweet words. The day following the king came to his son and began to clip, embrace and kiss him, and said to him, " My right sweet son, honour thou mine old age, son, dread thy father. Knowest thou not well that it is good to obey thy father and make him glad, and for to do contrary it is sin, and they that anger them sin evil?" To whom Josaphat said, " There is time to love, and time

to hate, time of peace, and time of battle, and
we ought in no wise love them nor obey to them
that would put us away from God, be it father or
mother." And when his father saw his stead-
fastness, he said to him, "Since I see thy folly,
and thou wilt not obey to me, come and we shall
know the truth. For Barlaam which hath deceived thee is bounden in my prison. And let
us assemble our people with Barlaam, and I shall
send for all the Galileans that they may safely
come without dread and dispute. And if that
ye with your Barlaam overcome us, we shall believe and obey you : and if we overcome you, ye
shall consent to us."

And this pleased well to the king and to Josaphat. And when they had ordained that he
that named him Barlaam should defend the
faith of Christ, and suffer him after to be overcome, and so were all assembled, then Josaphat
turned him toward Nachor, which feigned him to
be Barlaam, and said, "Barlaam thou knowest well
how thou hast taught me, and if thou defend the
faith that I have learned of thee, I shall abide in
thy doctrine to the end of my life. And if thou
be overcome, I shall avenge anon on thee mine
injury and shall pluck thy tongue out of thine
head with mine hands and give it to dogs, to the
end that thou be not so hardy to put a king's son
in error." And when Nachor heard that, he was
in great fear, and saw well that if he said contrary
he were but dead, and that he was taken in his
own snare. And then he advised that it were

better to take and hold with the son than with
the father, for to eschew the peril of death. For
the king had said to him before them all, that
he should defend the faith hardily and without
dread. Then one of the masters said to him,
"Thou art Barlaam which hast deceived the son
of the king." And he said "I am Barlaam which
hath not put the king's son in any error, but I
have brought him out of error." And then the
master said to him, " Right noble and marvellous
men have worshipped our gods, how darest thou
then address thee against them?" And he answered, "They of Chaldea, of Egypt and of
Greece, have heard and said that the creatures
were gods: and the Chaldees supposed that the
elements had been gods which were created to the
profit of men. And the Greeks supposed that
cursed men and tyrants had been gods, as Saturn
who they said ate his son, and Jupiter which as
they say gelded his father; and Jupiter to be king
of the other gods by cause he transformed oft himself in likeness of a beast for to accomplish his
adultery. And also they say that Venus is Goddess
of adultery, and sometimes Mars is her husband and
sometimes Adonis. The Egyptians worship the
beasts, that is to wit, a sheep, a calf, a swine or such
others. And the Christian men worship the Son
of the right high King, that descended from heaven and took nature human." And then Nachor
began clearly to defend the law of Christian men,
and garnished him with many reasons, so that the
masters were all abashed and wist not what to an-

swer. And then Josaphat had great joy of that our Lord had defended the truth by him that was enemy of truth. And then the king was full of woodness, and commanded that the council should depart; like as he would have treated again on the morrow of the same fact. Then Josaphat said to his father, "Let my master be with me this night to the end that we may make our collation together for to make to-morrow our answer; and thou shalt lead thy masters with thee and shalt take council with them; and if thou lead my master with thee thou doest me no right." Wherefore he granted to him Nachor by cause he hoped that he should deceive him. And when the king's son was come to his chamber and Nachor with him, Josaphat said to Nachor, "Ne wenest thou not that I know thee? I wot well that thou art not Barlaam, but thou art Nachor the astronomer." And Josaphat preached then to him the way of health, and converted him to the faith, and on the morn sent him into desert and there he was baptized and led the life of an hermit.

Then there was an enchanter named Theodas, when he heard of this thing he came to the king and said that he should make his son return and believe in his gods. And the king said to him, "If thou do so, I shall make to thee an image of gold and offer sacrifices thereto, like as to my gods." And he said, "Take away all them that be about thy son and put to him fair women and well adorned, and command them alway to abide by him. And after I shall send a wicked spirit that shall enflame him to luxury, and there is no thing that may so soon deceive the young men as the beauty of women." And he said yet more.

" There was a king which had with great pain a son, and the wise masters said that if he saw sun or moon within ten years he should lose the sight of his eyes. Then it was ordained that this child should be nourished within a pit made in a great rock. And when the ten years were passed, the king commanded that his son should be brought forth and that all things should be brought tofore him by cause he should know the names of those things. And then they brought tofore him jewels, horses and beasts of all manners, and also gold, silver, precious stones, and all other things. And when he had demanded the names of every thing, and that the ministers had told him, he set nought thereby. And when his father saw that he recked not of such things, then the king made to be brought tofore him women quaintly arrayed. And he demanded what they were. They would not so lightly tell him, whereof he was annoyed, and after the master squire of the king said japing, that they were devils that deceive men. Then the king demanded him what he lievest have of all that he had seen, and he answered, " Father my soul coveteth nothing so much as the devils that deceive men." " And therefore I suppose that none other thing shall surmount thy son but women, which move men all way to lechery."

Then the king put out all his ministers, and set therein to be about his son right noble and fair maidens, which alway him admonested to play, and there were none other that might speak nor serve him. And anon the enchanter sent to him the devil for to enflame him, which burned the young man withinforth, and the maidens withoutforth. And when he felt him so strongly travailed he was much angry, and recommended himself all to God, and he received divine comfort in such wise that all temptation departed from him.

And after this the king saw that the devil had done nothing and he sent to him a fair maiden, a king's daughter which was fatherless. To whom this man of God preached, and she answered, "If thou wilt save me, and take me away from worshipping the idols, conjoin thee unto me by coupling of marriage, for the patriarchs, prophets, and Peter the apostle had wives." And he said to her, "Woman these words sayest thou now for nought. It appertaineth well to Christian men to wed wives, but not to them that have promised to Our Lord to keep virginity." And she said to him, "Now be it as thou wilt; but if thou wilt save my soul grant to me a little request, lie with me only this night and I promise to thee that to morn I shall be made Christian. For, as ye say the angels have more joy in heaven of one sinner doing penance than for many other, there is great guerdon due to him that doth penance and converteth him. Therefore grant to me only this request, and so thou shalt save me." And then she began strongly to assail the tower

of his conscience. Then the devil said to his
fellows, "Go, see how this maid hath strongly
put forth that we might not move. Come then
and let us knock strongly against him since we
find now time convenable." And then the holy
young man saw this thing and that he was in that
caitiffness that the covetise of his flesh admonested him to sin, and also that he desired the sal-
vation of the maid by enticing of the devil that
moved him, he then put himself to prayer in
weeping. And there he fell a sleep and saw by
a vision that he was brought in to a meadow
arrayed with fair flowers, there where the leaves
of the trees demeaned a sweet sound which came
by a wind agreeable, and thereout issued a marvellous odour, and the fruit was right fair to see,
and right delectable of taste, and there were seats
of gold and silver and precious stones, and the
beds were noble and preciously adorned, and
right clear water ran thereby. And after that he
entered in to a city of which the walls were of
fine gold and shone by marvellous clearness, and
saw in the air some that sang a song that never
ear of mortal man heard like. And it was said,
"This is the place of blessed saints." And as
they would have had him thence, he prayed them
that they would let him dwell there. And they
said to him, "Thou shalt yet hereafter come
hither with great travail if thou mayest suffer."
And after they led him into a right horrible place
full of all filth and stench and said to him, "This
is the place of wicked people." And when he

awoke, him seemed that the beauty of that dam-
sel was more foul than all the ordure. And then
the wicked spirits came again to Theodas and he
blamed them, to whom they said, "We ran upon
him tofore he marked him with the sign of the
cross, and troubled him strongly, and when he was
garnished with the sign of the cross he persecuted
us with great force." Then Theodos came to
him with the king and had hoped that he should
have perverted him, but this enchanter was taken
of him whom he supposed to have taken, and
was converted and received baptism and lived
after an holy life.

And the king was all despaired, and by counsel
of his friends he delivered to him half his realm.
And how be it that Josaphat desired with all his
thought the desert, yet for to encrease the faith
he received the realm for a certain time, and
made churches and raised crosses and converted
much people of his realm to the faith of Jesus
Christ. And at last the father consented to the
reasons and predications of his son and believed
on the faith of Jesus Christ, and received baptism
and left his realm whole to his son and entended
to works of penance, and after finished his life
laudably.

And Josaphat oft warned the king Barachias
that he should go into the desert, but he was retained of the people long time. But at last he
fled away in to the desert, and as he went in
desert he gave to a poor man his habit royal and
abode in a right poor gown. And the devil made

to him many assaults, for sometime he ran upon
him with a sword drawn and menaced to smite if
he left not the desert; and another time he appeared to him in the form of a wild beast and
foamed and ran on him as he would have devoured him; and then Josaphat said: " Our Lord
is mine helper, I doubt no thing that man may
do to me."

And thus Josaphat was two years vagant and
erred in desert and could not find Barlaam. And
at the last he found a cave in the earth and
knocked at the door and said: " Father, bless
me." And anon Barlaam heard the voice of him
and rose up and went out. And then each
kissed other and embraced straitly, and were
glad of their assembling. And after, Josaphat
recounted to Barlaam all these things that were
happened, and he rendered and gave thankngs to
God therefore. And Josaphat dwelled there many
years in great and marvellous penance, full of virtues. And when Barlaam had accomplished his
days he rested in peace about the year of Our
Lord CCCC and LXXX. Josaphat left his realm
the xxv year of his age, and led the life of an
hermit five and thirty years and then rested in
peace, full of virtues, and was buried by the body
of Barlaam. And when the king Barachias heard
of this thing, he came unto that same place with a
great company and took the bodies and bore them
with much great honour in to his city, where
God hath shewed many fair miracles at the tomb
of these two precious bodies.

V.—THE VOYAGE OF SAINT BRANDON.

SAINT BRANDON, the holy man, was a monk and born in Ireland. And there he was Abbot of a house wherein were a thousand monks, and there he had a full straight and holy life in great penance and abstinence, and he governed his monks full virtuously. And then within short while after there came to him an holy Abbot, that hight Berinus, to visit him, and each of them was joyful of other. And then Saint Brandon began to tell to the Abbot Berinus of many wonders that he had seen in divers lands. And when Berinus heard that of Saint Brandon, he began to sigh and sore wept. And Saint Brandon comforted him in the best wise that he could, saying: "Ye come hither for to be joyful with me, and therefore for God's love leave your mourning, and tell me what marvels ye have seen in the great sea ocean that compasseth all the world about and all other waters come out of him, which runneth in all the parts of the earth."

And then Berinus began to tell to Saint Brandon and his monks the marvels that he had seen, full sore weeping. And said: "I have a son, his name is Mernoke. And he was a monk of great fame, which had great desire to seek about by ship in divers countries to find a solitary place wherein he might dwell secretly out of the business of the world for to serve God quietly and with more devotion. And I counselled him to sail into an island far in the sea beside the Mountain of Stones, which is full well known. And then he made him ready and sailed thither with his monks. And when he came thither he liked the place full well: where he and his monks served Our Lord full devoutly."

And then Berinus saw in a vision that this monk Mernoke was sailed right far eastward in the sea more than three days' sailing. And suddenly, to his seeming, there came a dark cloud and over-covered them that a great part of the day they saw no light. And as Our Lord would, the cloud passed away and they saw a full fair island and thitherward they drew. In that island was joy and mirth enough. And the earth of the island shined as bright as the sun; and there were the fairest trees and herbs that ever any man saw. And there were many precious stones shining bright, and every herb there was full of figures, and every tree full of fruit: so that it was a glorious sight, and a heavenly joy to abide there.

And then there came to them a fair young man, and full courteously he welcomed them all, and called every monk by his name. And he said that they were much bound to praise the name of Our Lord that would, of His grace, shew to them this glorious place where is ever day and never

c

night. And this place is called Paradise Terrestrial : but by this island is another island wherein no man may come. And this young man said to them : "Ye have been here half a year without meat, drink, or sleep," and they supposed they had not been there the space of half an hour, so merry and joyful they were. And the young man told them that this is the place that Adam and Eve dwelled in, and ever would have dwelled there if that they had not broken the commandment of God.

Then the young man brought them to their ship again and said they might no longer abide there. And when they were all shipped, suddenly this young man vanished away out of their sight. And then within short time after, by the purveyance of Our Lord, they came to the Abbey where they dwelled. And their brethren received them goodly and demanded them where they had been so long. And they said : "We have been in the Land of Behest,* tofore the gates of Paradise, whereas is ever day and never night." And they said all that the place is full delectable ; for yet all their clothes smelled of the sweet and joyful place.

And then Saint Brandon purposed soon after for to seek that place by God's help; and anon began to purvey for a good ship and a strong and victualled it for seven years. And then he took his leave of all his brethren and took twelve monks with him. But, or they entered into the ship, they fasted forty days and lived devoutly and each

* Promise.

of them received the Sacrament. And when
Saint Brandon with his twelve monks were entered into the ship, there came other two of his
monks and prayed him that they might sail with
him. And then he said : " Ye may sail with me,
but one of you shall go to Hell or ye come again."
But for all that they would go with him.

And then Saint Brandon had the shipmen to
wind up the sail, and forth they sailed in God's
name ; so that on the morrow they were out of
sight of any land. And forty days and forty
nights after they sailed into the East.

And then they saw an island far from them
and they sailed thitherward as fast as they could :
and they saw a great rock of stone appear above
all the water. And three days they sailed about
it or they could get into the place. But at the
last, by the purveyance of God, they found a little
haven and there went on land every one. And
then suddenly came a fair hound and fell down at
the feet of Saint Brandon and made him good
cheer in his manner. And then he bade his
brethren be of good cheer. " For Our Lord hath
sent to us his messenger to lead us into some good
place." And the hound brought them into a fair
hall, where they found the tables spread, ready
set full of good meat and drink. And then Saint
Brandon said graces, and then he and his brethren
sat down and ate and drank of such as they found.
And there were beds ready for them wherein they
took their rest after their long labour.

And on the morrow they returned again to their

ship, and sailed a long time in the sea after or they
could find any land : till at the last by the purveyance of Almighty God, they saw far from them
a full fair island full of green pasture, wherein
were the whitest and greatest sheep that ever they
saw ; for every sheep was as great as an ox. And
soon after came to them a goodly old man which
welcomed them and made to them good cheer, and
said "This is the Island of Sheep. And here is
never cold weather but ever summer and that
caused the sheep to be so great and white : they
eat of the best grass and herbs that is anywhere."
And then this old man took his leave of them and
bade them sail forthright east and within short
time by God's grace they should come to a place
like Paradise wherein they should keep their
Easter-tide.

And then they sailed forth and came soon after
to land but could find no haven because of little
depth in some place and in some place were
great rocks. But at the last they went upon an
island weening they had been safe, and made
thereon a fire for to dress their dinner. But Saint
Brandon abode still in the ship. When the fire
was right hot and the meat nigh sodden, then this
island began to move, whereof the monks were
afraid and fled anon to the ship and left the fire
and meat behind them. And Saint Brandon comforted them and said that it was a great fish named
Jasconius which laboured night and day to put his
tail in his mouth but for greatness he may not.

And then anon they sailed west three days and

three nights or they saw any land, wherefore they were right heavy. But soon after, as God would, they saw a fair island full of flowers, herbs and trees; whereof they thanked God of His good grace and anon they went on land. And when they had gone long in this, they found a full fair well and thereby stood a fair tree full of boughs. And on every bough sat a fair bird and they sat so thick on the tree that unneth any leaf of the tree might be seen, the number of them was so great. And they sang so merrily that it was an heavenly noise to hear.

Wherefore Saint Brandon kneeled down on his knees, and wept for joy, and made his prayers devoutly to Our Lord God to know what these birds meant. And then anon one of these birds fled from the tree to Saint Brandon, and with flickering of his wings made a full merry noise like a fiddle, that him seemed he heard never so joyful a melody. And then Saint Brandon commanded the bird to tell him the cause why they sat so thick on the tree and sung so merrily.

And then the bird said: "Sometime we were angels in Heaven. But when our master Lucifer fell down into Hell for his high pride, we fell with him for our offences, some higher and some lower, after the quality of their trespasses. And because our trespass is but little, therefore Our Lord hath set us here, out of all pain, in full great joy and mirth, after His pleasing, here to serve Him in this tree in the best manner that we can. This Sunday is a day of rest from all worldly occupation, and therefore this day all we be made as white as any snow for to praise Our Lord in the best wise we may." And then this bird said to Saint Brandon : "It is twelve months past that ye departed from your Abbey : and in the seventh year hereafter ye shall see the place that ye desire to come at. And all this seven years, ye shall keep your Easter here with us every year. And in the end of the seventh year, ye shall come unto the Land of Behest."

And this was on Easter-day that the bird said these words to Saint Brandon ; and then this fowl flew again to his fellows that sat on the tree. Then all the birds began to sing evensong so merrily that it was an heavenly sound to hear. And after supper, Saint Brandon and his fellows went to bed and slept well. On the morrow they arose betimes and then those birds began Matins, Prime and Hours and all such service as Christian men use to sing. And Saint Brandon with his fellows abode there eight weeks till Trinity Sunday was passed.

And they sailed again to the Island of Sheep, and they victualled them well and took their leave of that old man and returned again to ship. And then the bird of the tree came against Saint Brandon and said : "I am come to tell you that ye shall sail from hence into an island, where is an Abbey of twenty-four monks, which is from this place many a mile. There ye shall hold your Christmas : and your Easter with us like as I told you." And then this bird flew to his fellows again,

So Saint Brandon and his fellows sailed forth
in the ocean; and soon after fell a great tempest
on them in which they were greatly troubled
long time and sore for-laboured. And after that
they found by the purveyance of God an island
that was far from them, and then full meekly
they prayed to Our Lord to send them thither in
safety. But it was forty days after or they came
thither: wherefore all the monks were so weary
of that trouble that they set little price by their
lives, and cried continually to Our Lord to have
mercy on them and bring them to that island in
safety. And by the purveyance of God they
came in at the last into a little haven, but it was
so strait that unneth the ship might come in.

And after, they came to an anchor and anon
the monks went to land. And when they had
long walked about, at the last they found two fair
wells: one was fair and clear water, but the other
was somewhat troubled and thick. And then
they thanked Our Lord fully humbly that had
brought them thither in safety. And they would
fain have drunken of that water, but Saint Brandon charged them they should not take without
licence: "For if we abstain us awhile, Our Lord
will purvey for us in the best wise." And anon
after came to them a fair old man with hoar hair,
and welcomed them full meekly and kissed Saint
Brandon, and led them by many fair wells till
they came to a fair Abbey.

There they were received with great honour
and solemn procession with twenty-four monks

all in royal copes of cloth of gold, and a great cross was before them. And then the Abbot welcomed Saint Brandon and his fellowship and kissed them full meekly. Then he took Saint Brandon by the hand and led him with his monks into a fair hall and set them down in a row upon the bench. And the abbot of the place washed all their feet with fair water of the well that they saw before. After, he led them in to the fratour* and there set them among his convent. And anon there came one by the purveyance of God that served them with their meat and drink. For every monk had set before him a fair white loaf and white roots and herbs which were right delicious but they wist not what roots they were. And they drank of the water of the fair clear well which they saw before when they came first to land which Saint Brandon forbade them.

And the abbot came and cheered Saint Brandon and his monks and bade them eat and drink for charity. "For every day, Our Lord sendeth a goodly old man which covereth this table and setteth our meat and drink before us. We know not how it cometh and we ordain never meat nor drink for us, and yet we have been eighty years here, and ever Our Lord, worshipped mote He be, feedeth us. We be twenty-four monks in number and every ferial day of the week He sendeth to us twelve loaves and every Sunday and feastful day twenty-four loaves; and the bread that we leave at dinner we eat at supper. And

* Frater-house, refectory or hall of the monastery.

now at your coming Our Lord hath sent unto us forty-eight loaves for to make you and us merry together as brethren. And always twelve of us go to dinner while other twelve keep the choir. Thus have we done ·these eighty years for so long have we dwelled in this Abbey. We came hither out of the Abbey of Saint Patrick in Ireland and thus as ye see Our Lord hath purveyed for us. But none knoweth how it cometh but God alone to Whom be given honour and laud, world without end. Here in this land is ever fair weather and none of us hath ever been sick since we came hither. And when we go to Mass or to any other service of Our Lord in the church, anon seven tapers of wax are set in the choir and lit at every time without man's hand, and burn day and night at every hour of service, and have never wasted or minished as long as we have been here, which is eighty years."

Then Saint Brandon went to the church with the abbot of the place, and there they said Evensong together full devoutly. And then Saint Brandon looked upward towards the Crucifix and Our Lord hanging on the Cross which was made of fine crystal and curiously wrought. And in the choir were four-and-twenty seats for four-and-twenty monks, and the seven tapers burning; and the abbot's seat was made in the midst of the choir.

Then Saint Brandon demanded of the abbot how long they had kept that silence that none of them spake to other. And he said: "This four-

and-twenty years we spake never one to another."
And then Saint Brandon wept for joy of their
holy conversation. And then Saint Brandon desired of the abbot that he and his monks might
dwell there still with him. To whom the abbot
said: "Sir, that may ye not do in no wise. For
Our Lord hath shewed to you in what manner ye
shall be guided till the seven years be fulfilled.
Aud after that term thou shalt with thy monks
return into Ireland in safety. But one of the
two monks that came last to you shall dwell in
the Island of Ankers* and that other shall go
quick to hell."

And as Saint Brandon kneeled in the Church,
he saw a bright shining angel come in at the window, and lighted all the lights in the Church,
and then he flew out again at the window into
heaven. Then Saint Brandon marvelled greatly
how the light burned so fair and wasted not.
Then the Abbot said that it is written that Moses
saw a bush all on a fire and that it burned not:
"And therefore marvel not thereof for the might
of Our Lord is now as great as it ever was."

And when Saint Brandon had dwelled there
from Christmas even till the twelve days were
passed, then he took his leave of the Abbot of the
convent and returned with his monks to the ship.
And he sailed from thence with his monks on the
day of Saint Hilary. But they had great tempests
in the sea from that time till Palm Sunday.

And then they came to the Island of Sheep and

* Anchorites, hermits.

there were received of the old man, which brought them to a fair hall and served them. And on Shere-Thursday* after supper, he did wash all their feet and kissed them like as Our Lord did to His disciples. And there they abode till Saturday, Easter even.

And then they departed and sailed to the place where the fish lay. And anon they saw their cauldron upon the fish's back, which they had left there twelve months before. There they kept the service of the Resurrection, on the fish's back.

And after, they sailed that same day by the morning to the island whereas the tree of the birds was. And then the bird welcomed Saint Brandon and all his fellowship and went again to the tree and sang full merrily. And there, he and his monks dwelled from Easter till Trinity Sunday, as they did the year before, in full great joy and mirth. And daily they heard the merry service of the birds sitting on the tree.

And then the bird told to Saint Brandon that he should return again at Christmas to the Abbey of Monks, and at Easter thither again ; and the other part of the year labour in the ocean in full great perils. "And so from year to year till the seven years be accomplished. And then shall ye come to the joyful place of Paradise and dwell there forty days in full great joy and mirth. And after, ye shall return home into your own Abbey

* The Thursday before Easter. So called because on that day the monks used to shave their heads.

in safety, and there end your life and come to the bliss of Heaven to which Our Lord bought you with His precious Blood."

And then the angel of Our Lord ordained all thing that was needful to Saint Brandon and to his monks in victuals and all other things necessary. And then they thanked Our Lord of His great goodness He had shewed to them oft in their great need, and sailed forth in the great sea ocean abiding the mercy of Our Lord in great trouble and tempests. And soon after came to them an horrible fish which followed the ship long time casting forth much water out of his mouth into the ship that they supposed to have been drowned : wherefore they devoutly prayed God to deliver them of that great peril. And anon after came another fish, greater than he, out of the West sea and fought with him ; and at the last clave him into three pieces and returned again. And then they thanked meekly Our Lord for their deliverance from this great peril.

Then were they in great heaviness because their victuals were nigh spent. But by the ordinance of Our Lord, there came a bird and brought to them a great branch of a vine full of red grapes by which they lived fourteen days. And then they came to a little island wherein were many vines full of grapes. And they there landed and thanked God and gathered as many grapes as they lived by forty days after : alway sailing in the sea in many storms and tempests.

And as they thus sailed suddenly came flying

towards them a great gryphon which assailed them
and was like to have destroyed them.   Wherefore
they devoutly prayed for help and aid of Our
Lord Jesus Christ.   And then the bird of the tree
of the island where they had holden their Easter
to-fore came to the gryphon and smote out both
his eyes and after slew him.

And then they sailed forth continually till
Saint Peter's day, and then sung they solemnly
their service in the honour of the feast.   And in
that place the water was so clear that they might
see all the fishes that were about them ; whereof
they were full sore aghast.   And the monks
counselled Saint Brandon to sing no more : for
all the fishes lay then as they had slept.   And
then Saint Brandon said : " Dread ye not.   For
ye have kept by two Easters the Feast of the
Resurrection upon the great fish's back and therefore dread ye not of these little fishes."   And
then Saint Brandon made him ready and went to
Mass and bade his monks to sing the best wise
they could.   And then anon all the fishes awoke
and came about the ship so thick that unneth
they might see the water for the fishes.   And
when the Mass was done, all the fishes departed
so as they were no more seen.   And seven days
they sailed always in that clear water.

And then there came a south wind and drove
the ship northward whereas they saw an island
full dark and full of stench and smoke.   And
there they heard great blowing and blasting of
bellows but they might see nothing, and heard

great thundering: whereof they were sore afraid and blessed them oft. And soon after, there came one starting out all burning in fire and gazed full ghastly upon them with great staring eyes, of whom the monks were aghast. And at his departing from them he made the horriblest cry that might be heard. And soon there came a great number of fiends and assailed them with hooks and burning iron mallets, which ran on the water following their ship fast, in such wise that it seemed all the sea to be on fire. But by the pleasure of Our Lord, they had no power to hurt nor grieve them nor their ship: wherefore the fiends began to roar and cry and threw their hooks and mallets at them. And they then were sore afeard and prayed to God for comfort and help, for they saw the fiends all about the ship, and them seemed then all the island and the sea to be on a fire. Whereat with a sorrowful cry all the fiends departed from them and returned to the place that they came from. And then Saint Brandon told to them that this was a part of hell, and therefore he charged them to be stedfast in the faith for they should yet see many a dreadful place or they came home again.

And then came the south wind and drove them further to the north: where they saw an hill all on fire and a foul smoke and stench coming from thence: and the fire stood on each side of the hill, like a wall, all burning. And then one of his monks began to cry and weep full sore, and said that his end was come and that he might abide no longer in the ship. And anon he leapt out of the ship into the sea. And then he cried and roared full piteously, cursing the time that he was born and also the father and mother that begat him because they saw no better to his correction in his young age: "Wherefore now I must go to perpetual pain." And then the saying of the blessed Saint Brandon was verified that he said to him when he entered into the ship. Therefore it is good a man to do penance and forsake sin for the hour of death is uncertain.

And then anon the wind returned into the north and drove the ship into the south, which sailed seven days continually. And they came to a great rock standing in the sea: and thereon sat a naked man in full great misery and pain, for the waves of the sea had so beaten his body that all the flesh was gone off and nothing left but sinews and bare bones. And when the waves were gone, there was a canvas that hung over his head which beat his body full sore with the blowing of the wind. And also there were two ox-tongues and a great stone that he sat on which did him full great ease.

And then Saint Brandon charged him to tell him what he was. And he said: "My name is Judas, that sold Our Lord Jesus Christ for thirty pence, which sitteth here much wretchedly, howbeit I am worthy to be in the greatest pain that is. But Our Lord is so merciful that He hath rewarded me better than I have deserved; for of right my place is in the burning hell. But I am here but certain times of the year, that is, from Christmas till the twelfth day, and from Easter till Whitsuntide be past, and every feastful day of Our Lady, and every Saturday noon till on Sunday the evensong be done. But all other times, I lie still in hell in full burning fire with Pilate, Herod, and Caiaphas; therefore accursed be the time that ever I knew them."

And then Judas prayed Saint Brandon to abide still there all that night, and that he would keep him there still that the fiends should not fetch him to hell. And Saint Brandon said, "With God's help thou shalt abide here all this night." And then he asked Judas what cloth that was that hung over his head. And he said that it was a cloth that he gave to a leper, which was bought with the money that he stole from Our Lord when he bare His purse. "Wherefore, it doth to me full great pain now in beating my face with the blowing of the wind.* And these two ox-tongues that hang here above me I gave sometime to two priests to pray for me. Them I bought with mine own money, and therefore they ease me, because the fishes of the sea gnaw on them and spare me. And this stone that I sit on lay sometime in a desolate place where it eased no man. And I took it thence, and laid it in a foul way, where it did much ease to them that went by that way. And therefore it easeth

* And therefore let every man alive beware that he take away no man's good wrongfully for he shall suffer pain therefore. (From the manuscript used by Caxton.)

THE VOYAGE OF ST. BRANDON.

me now : for every good deed shall be rewarded,
and every evil deed shall be punished."

And then Sunday against even, there came a
great multitude of fiends blasting and roaring.
And they bade Saint Brandon go thence that
they might have their servant Judas : "For we
dare not come in the presence of our master, but
if we bring him to hell with us." And then said
Saint Brandon : "I hinder you not to do your
master's commandment, but by the power of the
Lord Jesus Christ, I charge you to leave him this
night till to-morrow." Thereto answered the
fiends : "How darest thou help him that so sold
his master for thirty pence and caused Him also
to die the most shameful death upon the cross ? "
And then Saint Brandon charged the fiends by
His Passion that they should not annoy him that
night. And then the fiends went their way,
roaring and crying, toward hell to their master
the Great Devil. And then Judas thanked Saint
Brandon so ruthfully that it was pity to see. And,
on the morrow, the fiends came with an horrible
noise, saying that they had that night suffered
great pain because they brought not Judas : and
said that he should suffer double pain the six days
following. And they took then Judas, trembling
for fear, with them to pain.

And after, the holy Saint Brandon sailed south-
ward, three days and three nights. And on the
Friday they saw an island. And then Saint Brandon began to sing; and said : "I see the island
wherein Saint Paul the hermit dwelleth, and hath

dwelled there forty years without meat and drink ordained by man's hand." And when they came to the land, Saint Paul came and welcomed them humbly. He was old and so forgrown with hair that no man might see his body. Of whom Saint Brandon said, weeping: "I see a man that liveth more like an angel than a man: wherefore we monks may be ashamed that we live not better." Then Saint Paul said to Saint Brandon: "Thou art better than I. For Our Lord hath shewed to thee more privities than he hath done to me: wherefore, thou oughtest to be more praised than I."

To whom Saint Paul said: "Some time I was a monk of Saint Patrick's Abbey in Ireland, and was guardian of the place whereas men enter into Saint Patrick's Purgatory. And on a day there came one to me and I asked him what he was." And he said: "I am your Abbot Patrick, and charge thee that thou depart from hence to-morrow early to the sea-side. And there thou shalt find a ship into which thou must enter, which God hath ordained for thee, Whose will thou must accomplish. And so the next day I arose and went forth, and found the ship, in which I entered. And, by the purveyance of God, I was brought into this island the seventh day after. And then I left the ship and went to land, and there I walked up and down a good while. And then, by the purveyance of God, there came an otter, going upon his hinder feet, and brought me a flint stone and an iron to strike fire with, in

the two fore-claws of his feet. And also, he had
about his neck great plenty of fishes, which he cast
down before me and went his way. And I smote
fire, and made a fire of sticks, and did seeth the
fish, by which I lived three days. And then the
otter came again and brought me fish for other
three days. And thus he hath done this fifty-one
years, through the grace of Almighty God. And
there was a great stone out of which Our Blessed
Lord made to spring fair water clear and sweet,
whereof I drink daily. And thus have I lived
one and fifty years. I was forty years old when
I came hither, and am now an hundred and nine
years old, and abide till it please Our Lord Jesus
Christ to send for me : and if it pleased Him, I
would fain be discharged of this wretched life."

And then he bad Saint Brandon to take of the
water of the well and to carry it into his ship.
"For it is time that thou depart, for thou hast a
great journey to do. For thou shalt sail to an
island which is forty days' sailing hence, where
thou shalt hold thine Easter like as thou hast done
to-fore, whereas the tree of birds is. And from
thence, thou shalt sail into the land of Behest and
shalt abide there forty days, and after return home
into thy country in safety." And then these holy
men took leave each of other, and they wept both
full sore and kissed each other.

And then the blessed Saint Brandon entered
into the ship, and sailed forty days ever South in
full great tempest. And on Easter Even they
came to their procurator which made to them

good cheer, as he had before-time. And from thence they came to the great fish where they said Matins and Mass on Easter Day. And when the Mass was done, the fish began to move, and swam forth fast into the sea, whereof the monks were sore aghast which stood upon him. For it was a great marvel to see such a fish as great as all a country for to swim so fast in the water. But, by the will of Our Blessed Lord, this fish set all the monks on land in the Paradise of Birds, all whole and sound, and then returned to the place that he came from. And then Saint Brandon and his monks thanked Our Lord God of their deliverance from the great fish, and kept their Eastertide till Trinity-Sunday, as they had done before-time.

And, after this, they took their ship and sailed forty days. And at the forty days' end, it began to hail right fast. And therewith came a dark mist which lasted long after: which feared Saint Brandon and his monks, and they prayed to Our Lord to keep and help them. And then anon came their procurator and bad them to be of good cheer: for they were come into the Land of Behest.

And soon after the mist passed away. And anon they saw the fairest country Eastward that any man might see and was so clear and bright that it was an heavenly sight to behold. And all the trees were charged with ripe fruit and the herbs were full of flowers. In which land they walked forty days but they could not see none end

of that land. And there was always day and
never night and the land attempered neither to hot
nor to cold.

And at the last they came to a fair river: but
they durst not go over. And there came to them
a fair young man, and welcomed them courteously
and did great reverence to Saint Brandon. And
he said to them : "Be ye now joyful. For this is
the land that ye have sought. But Our Lord wills
that ye depart hence hastily, and He will show you
more of His secrets. When ye come again unto
the sea, Our Lord wills that ye lade your ship with
the fruit of this land and hie you hence : for ye
may no longer abide here. But thou shalt sail
again to thine own country and soon after thou
comest home thou shalt die. And this water that
thou seest here departeth the world asunder. For
on the other side of this water may no man come
that is in this life. And the fruit that ye see here
is always thus ripe ; and always it is here light as
ye now see. And he that keepeth Our Lord's
hests at all times shall see this land or he pass out
of this world."

And then Saint Brandon and his monks took of
the fruit as much as they would ; and also took
with them great plenty of precious stones. And
they took their leave, and went to ship weeping
sore because they might no longer abide there.
And then they took their ship and came home into Ireland in safety, whom their bretheren received
with great joy, giving thankings to Our Lord,
which had kept them all these seven years from

many a peril and brought them home in safety.
To whom be given honour and glory, world without end, Amen.

And soon after this holy man, Saint Brandon,
waxed feeble and sick and had little joy of this
world, but ever after his joy and mind was in the
joys of heaven.   And in short time after, he, being
full of virtues, departed out of this life to everlasting life.   And he was worshipfully buried in
a fair Abbey, which he himself founded : where
Our Lord shewed for this holy saint many fair
miracles.   Wherefore let us devoutly pray to this
holy saint that he pray for us to Our Lord that He
have mercy on us.   To whom be given laud, honour, and empire, world without end, Amen.

VI.—THE LEGEND OF SAINT CHRISTOPHER.

CHRISTOPHER tofore his baptism was named Reprobus. But afterwards he was named Christopher which is as much to say, as bearing Christ. He bare Christ in four manners, he bare him on his shoulders, in his body by making it lean, in mind by devotion, and in his mouth by confession.

Christopher was of the lineage of the Canaaneans and he was of a right great stature, and had a terrible and fearful cheer and countenance. And he was twelve cubits of length. And, as it is read in some histories, when he served and dwelled with the king of Canaaneans, it came in his mind that he would seek the greatest prince that was in the world and him he would serve and obey.

And so far he went that he came to a right great king, of whom the renown generally was that he was the greatest of the world. And when the king saw him he received him into his service and made him to dwell in his court.

Upon a time a minstrel sung tofore him a song in which he named oft the devil. And the king, which was a Christian man, when he heard him name the devil, made anon the sign of the cross in his visage. And when Christopher saw that, he had great marvel what sign it was and wherefore the king made it. And he demanded it of him. And because the king would not say, he said, "If thou tell me not, I shall no longer dwell with thee." And then the king told to him saying, "Alway when I hear the devil named, I fear that he should have power over me, and I garnish me with this sign that he grieve not nor annoy me." Then Christopher said to him, "Thou doubtest the devil that he hurt thee not, then is the devil more mighty and greater than thou art. I am then deceived of my hope and purpose; for I supposed that I had founden the most mighty and the most greatest lord of the world. But I commend thee to God for I will go seek him to be my lord and I his servant."

And then he departed from this king and hasted him to seek the devil. And as he went by a great desert he saw a great company of knights. Of which a knight cruel and horrible came to him and demanded whither he went. And Christopher answered to him and said, "I go to seek the devil for to be my master." And he said, "I am he that thou seekest." And then Christopher was glad and bound himself to be his servant perpetual, and took him for his master and lord.

And as they went together by a common way, they found there a cross erect and standing. And anon as the devil saw the cross he was afeard and fled, and left the right way and brought Christopher about by a sharp desert, and after, when they were past the cross, he brought him to the highway that they had left. And when Christopher saw that, he marvelled and demanded whereof he doubted that he had left high and fair way and had gone so far about by so hard desert. And the devil would not tell to him in no wise. Then Christopher said to him, "If thou wilt not tell me I shall anon depart from thee and shall serve thee no more." Wherefore the devil was constrained to tell him, and said, "There was a man called Christ which was hanged on the cross, and when I see his sign, I am sore afeard and flee from it wheresomever I find it." To whom Christopher said, "Then he is greater and more mightier than thou, when thou art afeard of his sign. And I see well that I have laboured in vain since I have not founden the greatest lord of all the earth. And I will serve thee no longer. Go thy way then: for I will go seek Jesus Christ."

And when he had long sought and demanded where he should find Christ, at the last he came into a great desert to an hermit that dwelled there. And this hermit preached to him of Jesus Christ and informed him in the faith diligently. And he said to him "This king whom thou desirest to serve, requireth this service that thou must oft fast."

And Christopher said to him "Require of me some other thing and I shall do it. For that which thou requirest I may not do." And the hermit said "Thou must then wake and make many prayers." And Christopher said to him "I wot not what it is. I may do no such thing." And then the hermit said unto him "knowest thou such a river in which many be perished and lost?" To whom Christopher said, "I know it well." Then said the hermit "Because thou art noble and high of stature and strong in thy members, thou shalt be resident by that river and shalt bear over all them that shall pass there. Which shall be a thing right convenable to Our Lord Jesus Christ, whom thou desirest to serve, and I hope He shall shew Himself to thee." Then said Christopher, "Certes, this service may I well do, and I promise to Him for to do it."

Then went Christopher to this river, and made there his habitation for him. And he bare a great pole in his hand instead of a staff, by which he sustained him in the water: and bare over all manner of people without ceasing. And there he abode, thus doing many days.

And on a time, as he slept in his lodge, he heard the voice of a child which called him and said, "Christopher, come out and bear me over." Then he awoke and went out; but he found no man. And when he was again in his house, he heard the same voice, and he ran out and found no body. The third time he was called, and came thither, and found a child beside the rivage of the river :

ST. CHRISTOPHER.

which prayed him goodly to bear him over the
water. And then Christopher lift up the child
on his shoulders and took his staff and entered in
to the river for to pass. And the water of the
river arose and swelled more and more. And the
child was heavy as lead. And always as he went
further the water increased and grew more, and
the child more and more waxed heavy : in so much
that Christopher had great anguish and feared
to be drowned. And when he was escaped with
great pain and passed the water, and set the child
a ground, he said to the child, "Child, thou hast
put me in great peril. Thou weighest almost as
I had had all the world upon me. I might bear
no greater burden." And the child answered
"Christopher, marvel thou no thing. For thou
hast not only borne all the world upon thee ; but
thou hast borne Him that created and made all
the world upon thy shoulders. I am Jesus Christ,
the king to whom thou servest in this work. And
that thou mayest know that I say to thee truth,
set thy staff in the earth by the house, and thou
shalt see to-morrow that it shall bear flowers and
fruit." And anon he vanished from his eyes.

And then Christopher set his staff in the earth
and when he arose on the morrow, he found his
staff like a palm-tree bearing flowers, leaves and
dates.

And then Christopher went into the city of
Lycia and understood not their language ; then
he prayed Our Lord he might understand them :
and so he did. And as he was in this prayer, the

judges supposed that he had been a fool, and left him there. And when Christopher understood the language, he covered his visage and went to a place where they martyred Christian men, and comforted them in Our Lord. And then the judges smote him in the face. And Christopher said to them : "If I were not Christian, I would anon avenge mine injury." And then Christopher pitched his rod in the earth and prayed to Our Lord that, for to convert the people, it might bear flowers and fruit. And anon it did so, and then he converted eight thousand men. And then the king sent two knights for to fetch him to him. And they found him praying and durst not tell to him so. And anon after, the king sent as many more. And they anon set them down for to pray with him. And when Christopher arose, he said to them : "What seek ye ?" And when they saw him in the visage, they said to him : "The king hath sent us that we should lead thee bounden unto him." And Christopher said to them : "If I would, ye should not lead me to him bounden nor unbounden." And they said to him : "If thou wilt go thy way, go quit where thou wilt, and we shall say to the king that we have not found thee." "It shall not be so," said he, "but I shall go with you." And then he converted them in the faith ; and he commanded them that they should bind his hands behind his back and lead him so bounden to the king.

And when the king saw him, he was afeared and fell down off his siege. And his servants lifted him up, and then the king enquired his name and his country. And Christopher said to him: "Tofore or I was baptized, I was named Reprobus and now am named Christopher: tofore baptism a Canaanean, now a Christian man." To whom the king said: "Thou hast a foolish name, that is to wit of Christ crucified which could not help Himself ne may not profit to thee. Therefore, thou cursed Canaanean, why wilt thou not do sacrifice to our gods?" To whom Christopher said: "Thou art rightfully called Dagnus for thou art the death of the world and the fellow of the devil; and thy gods be made with the hands of men." And the king said to him: "Thou wert nourished among wild beasts, and therefore thou mayest not say but wild language and words unknown to men. And if thou wilt now do sacrifice to the gods, I shall give to thee great gifts and great honours. And if not I shall destroy thee and consume thee by great pains and torments." But for all this he would in no wise do sacrifice: wherefore he was sent into prison. And the king did do behead the knights that he had sent for him, whom he had converted.

And at the last the king commanded that he should be bounden to a strong stake and that he should be shot through with arrows by forty knights, archers. But none of all the knights might attain nor hurt him, for the arrows hung in the air nigh about him without touching. Then the king weened that he had been through shotten with the arrows of the knights, and addressed him

tor to go to him. And one of the arrows returned
suddenly from the air and smote him in the eye
and blinded him. To whom Christopher said :
."Tyrant, I shall die to-morrow. Make a little
clay with my blood tempered, and anoint therewith thine eye, and thou shalt receive health."
Then by the commandment of the king, he was
led for to be beheaded, and then there he made
his orison and his head was smitten off, and so he
suffered martyrdom. And the king then took a
little of his blood and laid it on his eye and said,
" In the name of God and of Saint Christopher,"
and was anon healed. Then the king believed in
God and gave commandment that if any person
blamed God or Saint Christopher he should anon
be slain with the sword.

VII.—THE LEGEND OF SAINT EUSTACE.

USTACE was named tofore his baptism Placidus, which is as much to say as pleasant to God. And Eustace is said of u that is to say good, and stachis that is, fortune. Therefore Eustace is, as it were, good fortune. He was pleasant to God in his conversation, and after, he held him in good works.

Eustace which first was named Placidus, was master of the chivalry of Trajan the Emperor, and was right busy in the works of mercy but he was a worshipper of idols. And he had a wife of the same rite and also of the deeds of mercy. Of whom he had two sons which he did do nourish after his estate. And because he was ententive to the work of mercy, he deserved to be enlumined to the way of truth. So that on a day as he was on hunting, he found an herd of harts, among whom he saw one more fair and greater than the others, which departed from the company and sprang into the thickest of the forest. And the other knights ran after the other harts, but Placidus sued him with all his might and enforced to take him. And when the hart saw

that he followed him with all his power, at the
last he went up on an high rock.   And Placidus
approaching nigh, thought in his mind how he
might take him.   And as he beheld and considered the hart diligently, he saw between his
horns the form of the holy cross shining more
clearer than the sun, and the image of Christ
which by the mouth of the hart (like as sometime
Balaam by the ass) spake to him saying, "Placidus,
wherefore followest thou me hither?   I am appeared to thee in this beast for the grace of thee.
I am Jesus Christ whom thou honourest ignor-
antly.   Thine alms be ascended up tofore me
and therefore I come hither so that by this hart
that thou huntest I may hunt thee."   And some
other say that this image of Jesus Christ which
appeared between the horns of the hart said these
words.   And when Placidus heard that, he had
great dread and descended from his horse to the
ground.   And an hour after he came to himself,
and arose from the ground and said, "Rehearse
again this that thou hast said and I shall believe
thee."   And then Our Lord said, "I am Jesus
Christ that formed heaven and earth, which made
the light to increase and divided it from darkness,
and established time, days and hours; which
formed man of the slime of the earth; which
appeared in earth in flesh for the health of the
lineage human; which was crucified, dead, buried
and rose the third day.   And when Placidus heard
this he fell down again to the earth and said, "I
believe, Lord, that Thou art He that made all

ST. EUSTACE.

things and convertest them that err." And Our Lord said to him, "If thou believest, go to the bishop of the city and do thee to be baptised." And Placidus said to Him, "Lord, wilt Thou that I hide this thing from my wife and my sons?" And Our Lord said to him, "Tell to them, that they also make themselves clean with thee. And see that thou come again to-morrow hither that I may appear again to thee, and may shew to thee that which shall come hereafter to thee."

And when he was come home to his house and told this thing to his wife in their bed, she cried, "My lord," and said, "And I saw Him this night that is passed and He said to me, 'To-morrow, thou, thy husband and thy sons shall come to me;' and now I know that it was Christ." Then they went to the bishop of Rome at midnight, which baptized them with great joy and named Placidus Eustace and his wife Theospita.

And on the morrow Eustace went to hunt as he did tofore, and when he came nigh to the place, he departed his knights as for to find venison. And anon he saw in the place the form of the first vision. And anon he fell down to the ground tofore the figure and said, "Lord, I pray Thee to shew to me that which Thou hast promised to me Thy servant." To whom Our Lord said, "Eustace, thou art blessed, which hast taken the washing of grace. For now thou hast surmounted the devil which had deceived thee and hast trodden him under foot. Now thy faith shall appear. The devil, because thou hast forsaken him, is armed cruelly against thee, and it behoveth thee to suffer many things and pains. For to have the crown of victory, thou must suffer much to humble thee from the high vanity of the world and shalt afterwards be enhanced in spiritual riches. Thou therefore fail not nor look not unto thy first glory. For thee behoveth that by temptations thou be another Job. And when thou shalt so be humbled, I shall come to thee and shall restore thee unto the first joy. Say to me now whether thou wilt now suffer and take temptations, or in the end of thy life." And Eustace said to Him, "Lord, if it so behoveth, command that temptation come to me now. But I beseech Thee to grant to me the virtue of patience." To whom Our Lord said, "Be thou constant, for My grace shall keep yonr souls." Then Our Lord ascended into heaven, and Eustace returned home and shewed all this to his wife.

After this a few days, the pestilence assailed his servants and his knights and slew them all. And in a little while after all his horses and his beasts died suddenly. And after this some that had been his fellows seeing his depredation, entered into his house by night and robbed him and bare away gold and silver and despoiled him of all other things. And he, his wife and children thanked God and fled away all naked. And because they doubted shame they fled away into Egypt and all his great possession came to nought by ravine of wicked people. Then the king and all his senators sorrowed much for the master of the chivalry which was so noble, because they might hear no tidings of him.

And as they went, they approached the sea, and found a ship and entered into it for to pass. And the master of the ship saw that the wife of Eustace was right fair and desired much for to have her. And when they were passed over he demanded his reward for their freight. And they had not whereof to pay : so that the master of the ship commanded that the wife should be holden and retained for his hire. And when Eustace heard that he gainsaid it long. Then the master of the ship commanded his mariners to cast him into the sea. And when Eustace saw that, he left his wife much sorrowfully, and took his two children and went weeping.

And thus sorrowing, he and his children came to a river, and for the great abundance of water he durst not pass that river with both his sons at once, which were then young. But at the last he left one of them on the brink of the river and bare over that other on his shoulders. And when he had passed the river he set down on the ground the child that he had borne over, and hasted him to fetch that other that he had left on the other side of the river And when he was in the midst of the water, there came a wolf and took the child that he had borne over, and fled withal to the wood. And he then all despaired of him, went for to fetch that other. And as he

went there came a great lion and bare away the
other child so that he might not retain him : for
he was in the middle of the river.   And then he
began to weep and draw his hair and would have
drowned himself in the water if the divine purveyance had not letted him.

And the herdmen and ploughmen saw the lion
bearing the child all alive, and they followed him
with their dogs : so that by divine grace the lion
left the child all safe without hurt.   And other
ploughmen cried and followed the wolf, and with
their staves and falchions delivered the child
whole and sound from his teeth without hurt.
And so both the herdmen and ploughmen were
of one village and nourished these children among
them.

And Eustace knew no thing thereof, but weeping and sorrowing, said to himself, " Alas, woe is
me ; for tofore this mishap I shone in great
wealth like a tree, but now I am naked of all
things.   Alas, I was accustomed to be accompanied with a great multitude of knights and
I am now alone and am not suffered to have my
sons.   O Lord, I remember me that Thou saidst
to me, 'Thee behoveth to be tempted as Job
was.'   But I see that in me is more done to than
was to Job.   For he lost all his possessions but he
had a dunghill to sit on, but to me is nothing
left.   He had friends which had pity on him and
I have none ; but wild beasts have borne away
my sons.   To him was his wife left and my wife
is taken from me and delivered to another.   O

good Lord, give Thou rest to my tribulations, and keep Thou so my mouth that my heart decline not into no words of malice and I be cast from thy visage." And thus saying and walking in great weeping, he went in to a street of the town, and there was hired for to keep the fields of the men of the town.

And so he kept them xv year. His sons were nourished in another town and knew not that they were brethren. And Our Lord kept the wife of Eustace so that the strange man had not to do with her nor touched her, but died and ended his life.

In that time the Emperor and the people were much tormented of their enemies and then they remembered of Placidus how he many times had fought nobly against them. For whom the Emperor was much sorrowful and sent out into divers parts many knights to seek him, and promised to them that found him much riches and great honour. And two knights which had been under him in chivalry came in to the same street where he dwelled. And anon as Placidus saw them he knew them. And then he remembered his first dignity and began to be heavy and said, "Lord, I beseech Thee, grant to me that I may sometime see my wife. For as for my sons I know well that they be devoured of wild beasts." And then a voice came to him and said, "Eustace, have thou good affiance, for anon thou shalt recover thine honour and shalt have thy wife and children." And anon he went with these knights and they knew him not but demanded of him if he knew any strange man named Placidus that had a wife and two children. And he said, "Nay." Yet he had them home to his hostel and served them. And when he remembered of his first estate he might not hold him from weeping. Then he went out and washed his face and returned for to serve them. And they considered and said that one to that other how that this man resembleth much to him that we seek. And that other answered, "Certainly, he is like unto him. Now let us see if he have a wound in his head that he gat in a battle." Then they beheld and saw the sign of the wound and they wist well that it was he that they sought. Then they arose and kissed him and demanded of his wife and children : and he said that his sons were dead and his wife was taken away from him : and then the neighbours ran for to hear this thing, because the knights told and recounted his first glory and his virtue. And they said to him the commandment of the Emperor and clad him with noble vestments.

Then after the journey of xv days, they brought him to the Emperor. And when he heard of his coming he ran anon against him and when he saw him he kissed him. Then Eustace recounted tofore them all by order that which had happened to him : and he was re-established unto the office to be again master of the chivalry and was constrained to do the office like as he did tofore.

And then he counted how many knights there were and saw that there were but few as to the regard of their enemies and commanded that all the young men should be gathered in the cities and towns. And it happed that the country where his sons were nourished should make and send two men of arms. Then all the inhabitants of that country ordained these two young men his sons most convenable above all other for to go with the master of the chivalry. And then when the master saw these two young men of noble form, adorned honestly with good manners, they pleased him much. And he ordained that they should be with the first of his table.

Then he went thus to the battle. And when he had subdued his enemies to him, he made his host to rest iii. days in a town where his wife dwelled and kept a poor hostelry. And these two young men, by the purveyance of God, were lodged in the habitation of their mother without knowing what she was. And on a time about midday, they spake that one to that other of their infancy and their mother which was there hearkened what they said much ententively. So the greatest said to the less, "When I was a child, I remember none other thing save that my father, which was master of the knights, and my mother which was right fair, had two sons, that is to say, me and another younger than I. And they took us and went out of their house by night and entered into a ship for to go I wot not whither. And when we went out of the ship our mother was left in the ship, I wot not in what manner. But my father bore me and my brother sore weeping. And when he came to a water he passed over with my younger brother and left me on the bank of the water. And when he returned a wolf came and bare away my brother: and ere my father might come to me, a great lion issued out of the forest, and took me up and bare me into the wood. But the herdmen that saw him took me from the mouth of the lion and I was nourished in such a town as ye know well. But I could never know what happened to my brother nor where he is." And when the younger heard this, he began to weep and say, "Forsooth like as I hear I am thy brother. For they that nourished me said that they had taken me from a wolf." And then they began to embrace and kiss each other and weep.

And when their mother had heard all this thing, she considered long in herself if they were her two sons, because they had said by order what was befallen them. And the next day following she went to the master of the chivalry and required him, saying, "Sir, I pray thee that thou command that I be brought again to my country. For I am of the country of the Romans and here I am a stranger." And in saying these words, she saw in him signs and knew by them that he was her husband. And then she might no longer forbear but fell down at his feet and said to him, "Sir, I pray thee to tell of thy first

estate, for I ween that thou art Placidus master of
the knights which otherwise art called Eustace
whom Jesus Christ converted and hast suffered
such temptation and such. And I that am thy
wife was taken from thee on the sea, which
nevertheless have been kept from all corruption.
And thou hadst of me two sons, Agapetus and
Theospitus." And Eustace hearing this diligently considered and beheld her and anon knew
that she was his wife. And he wept for joy and
kissed her and glorified much our Lord God
which comforted the discomforted. And then
said his wife, "Sir, where be our sons?" And
he said that they were slain of wild beasts and he
recounted to her how he had lost them. And
she said, "Let us give thankings to God: for I
I suppose that like as God has given to us grace
each to find other so shall He give us grace to
recover our sons." And he said, "I have told
to thee that they be devoured of wild beasts."
And she then said, "I sat yesterday in a garden
and heard two younglings thus and thus ex-
pounding their infancy, and I believe that they
be our sons. Demand them and they shall tell
to thee the truth." Then Eustace called them
and heard their infancy and knew that they were
his sons. Then he embraced them and the
mother also and kissed them. Then all the host
enjoyed strongly of the finding of his wife and
children, and for the victory of the barbarians.

And when he was returned, Trajan was then
dead and Hadrian succeeded in the Empire which

was worst in all felonies. And as well for the victory, as for the finding of his wife and children, he received them much honourably, and did do make a great dinner and feast. And on the next day after he went to the temple of the idols for to sacrifice for the victory of the barbarians. And then the Emperor seeing that Eustace would not do sacrifice, neither for the victory nor for that he had found his wife and children, warned and commanded him that he should do sacrifice. To whom Eustace said, "I adore and do sacrifice to Our Lord Jesus Christ and only serve Him." And then the Emperor, replenished with ire, put him, his wife, and his sons in a certain place and did do go to them a right cruel lion. And the lion ran to them and inclined his head to them, like as he had worshipped them, and departed. Then the Emperor did do make a fire under an ox of brass or copper: and when it was fire hot, he commanded that they should be put therein all quick and alive. And then the saints prayed and commended them unto Our Lord, and entered into the ox and there yielded up their spirits to Jesus Christ. And the third day after they were drawn out tofore the Emperor, and were found all whole and not touched by the fire, nor as much as an hair of them was burnt, nor none other thing on them. And then the the Christian men took the bodies of them and laid them in a right noble place honourably and made over them an oratory. And they suffered death under Hadrian the Emperor, which began about the year of Our Lord CXX, in the kalends of November.

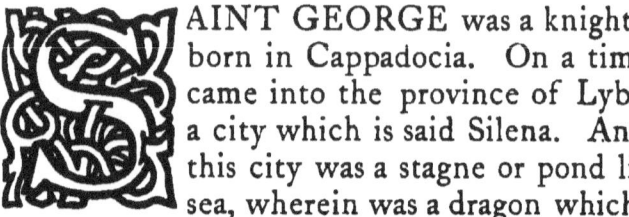

AINT GEORGE was a knight and born in Cappadocia. On a time he came into the province of Lybia to a city which is said Silena. And by this city was a stagne or pond like a sea, wherein was a dragon which envenomed all the country. And on a time the people were assembled for to slay him. And when they saw him they fled, and when he came nigh the city, he venomed the people with his breath. And therefore the people of the city gave to him every day two sheep for to feed him, by cause he should do no harm to the people. And when the sheep failed there was taken a man and a sheep. Then was an ordinance made in the town that there should be taken the children and young people of them of the town by lot, and every one as it fell, were he gentle or poor, should be delivered when the lot fell on him or her.

So it happened that many of them of the town were then delivered, in so much that the lot fell upon the king's daughter. Whereof the king was sorry and said to the people, "For the love of the gods take gold and silver and all that I have, and let me have my daughter." They said, "Sir, ye

SAINT GEORGE

have made and ordained the law and our children
be now dead; and now ye would do the contrary.
Your daughter shall be given or else we shall burn
you and your house."

When the king saw he might no more do, he
began to weep and said to his daughter, "Now
shall I never see thine espousals." Then returned
he to his people and demanded eight days respite
and they granted it to him. And when the eight
days were passed, they came to him and said
"Thou seest that the city perisheth." Then did
the king do array his daughter like as she should
be wedded, and embraced her and kissed her, and
gave her his benediction, and after led her to the
place where the dragon was.

When she was there, Saint George passed by
and when he saw the lady, he demanded the lady
what she made there. And she said, "Go ye your
way, fair young man, that ye perish not also."
Then said he, "Tell to me why ye weep and
doubt ye no thing." When she saw that he
would know, she said to him how she was delivered to the dragon. Then said Saint George,
"Fair daughter, doubt ye no thing hereof for I
shall help thee in the name of Jesus Christ." She
said, "For God's sake, good knight, go your way
and abide not with me, for ye may not deliver
me."

Thus as they spake together, the dragon appeared and came running to them. And Saint
George was upon his horse and drew out his
sword, and garnished him with the sign of the

cross, and rode hardily against the dragon which came toward him, and he smote him with his spear and hurt him right sore and threw him to the ground.

And after he said to the maid, "Deliver to me your girdle and bind it about the neck of the dragon and be not afeard." When she had done so, the dragon followed her as it had been a meek beast and debonair.

Then she led him into the city. And the people fled by mountains and valleys and said, "Alas, alas, we shall all be dead." Then Saint George said to them, "Ne doubt ye no thing; without more, believe me in Jesus Christ and do ye to be baptized, and I shall slay the dragon." Then the king was baptized and all his people. And Saint George slew the dragon and smote off his head and commanded that he should be thrown in the fields. And they took four carts with oxen that drew him out of the city.

Then there were well fifteen thousand men baptized without women and children. And the king did do make a church there of Our Lady and of Saint George, in the which yet riseth a fountain of living water which healeth sick people that drink thereof. After this the king offered to Saint George as much money as might be numbered but he refused all and commanded that it should be given to poor people for God's sake. And he enjoined the king four things, that is, that he should have charge of the churches, and that he should honour the priests and hear their service diligently, and that he should have pity on the poor peop'e; and after kissed the king and departed.

It is found in the history of Antioch, that when the Christian men went over sea to conquer Jerusalem, that one, a right fair young man, appeared to a priest of the host and counselled him that he should bear with him a little of the relics of Saint George, for that Saint George was conductor of the battle. And so he did so much that he had some. And when it so was that they had assieged Jerusalem, and durst not mount nor go up on the walls for the quarrels and defence of the Saracens, they saw apertly Saint George, which had white arms with a red cross, that went up tofore them on the walls, and they followed him. And so was Jerusalem taken by his help.

GILES in English and Egidius in Latin. And it is said of E that is without, and geos, that is earth, and dya that is clear or godly. He was without earth by despising of earthly things, clear by enlumining of science, divine or godly by love which assembleth the lover to him that is loved.

Saint Giles was born in Athens, and was of noble lineage and royal kindred, and in his childhood he was informed in holy lecture. And on a day, as he went to the church, he found a sick man, which lay all sick in the way and demanded alms of Saint Giles, which gave him his coat : and as soon as he clad him withal he received full and entire health. And after that anon, his father and his mother died, and rested in Our Lord. And then Saint Giles made Jesus Christ heir of his heritage.

Then Giles doubted the peril of the world, and went secretly to the rivage of the sea, and saw there mariners in great peril, and like to perish in the sea. And he made his prayer, and anon the tempest ceased, and the mariners came to land and thanked God. And he understood by them that they went to Rome, and he desired

to go with them. Whom they received into their
ship gladly, and said they would have him go
thither without any freight or hire.

And then he came to Arles, and abode there
two years with Saint Caesarius, bishop of the
city, and there healed a man that had been sick
of the fevers three years.

And after he desired to go into desert and departed covertly and dwelled there long with an
hermit that was an holy man. And there by his
merits he chased away the sterility and barrenness
that was in that country and caused great plenty
of goods.

And when he had done this miracle, he doubted
the peril of the glory human, and left that place
and entered further into the desert. And there
he found a pit, and a little well, and a fair hind
which without doubt was purveyed of God for
to nourish him, and at certain hours ministered
her milk unto him.

And on a time servants of the king rode on
hunting and much people and many hounds with
them. It happed that they espied this hind and
they thought that she was so fair, that they followed her with hounds. And when she was sore
constrained, she fled for succour to the feet of
Saint Giles whom she nourished. And then he
was much abashed when he saw her so chafed
and more than she was wont to be: and then he
leapt up and espied the hunters. Then he prayed
to Our Lord that like as He sent her to him for
to be nourished by her, that He would save her.

Then the hounds durst not approach her by the space of a stone's cast, but they howled together and returned to the hunters. And then the night came, and they returned home again and took nothing.

And when the king heard say of this thing he had suspicion what it might be, and went and warned the bishop. And both went together with a great multitude of hunters. And when the hounds were on the place whereas the hind was, they durst not go forth as they did before. Then all they environed the bush for to see what there was. But that bush was so thick that no man nor beast might enter therein for the brambles and thorns that were there. And then one of the knights drew up an arrow foolishly for to make the hind afeard and leap out : but he wounded and hurt the holy man which ceased not to pray for the hind. And after this the hunters made a way with their swords and went unto the pit and saw there this ancient man, which was clothed in the habit of a monk of a right honourable figure and parure, and the hind lying by him. And the king and the bishop went alone to him and demanded him from whence he was, and what he was, and why he had taken so great a thickness of desert and of whom he was so hurt. And he answered right honestly to every demand. And when they had heard him speak, they thought that he was an holy man and required him humbly of pardon.

And they sent to him masters and surgeons for to

heal his wound and offered him many gifts. But he would never lay medicine to his wound nor receive their gifts, but refused them, and he prayed Our Lord that he might never be whole thereof in his life. For he knew well that virtue should profit to him in infirmity. And the king visited him oft and received of him the pasture of health: and the king offered him great riches but he refused all.

And after he admonished the king that he should do make a monastery, whereas the discipline of the order of monks should be. And when he had do make it, Giles refused many times to take the charge. And at the last he was vanquished by prayers of the king and took it.

And then King Charles heard speak of the renown of him, and besought that he might see him: and he received him much honourably. And he prayed him to pray for him, among other things by cause he had done a sin so foul and villanous that he durst not be shriven thereof to him, or to none other. And on the Sunday after, as Saint Giles said Mass and prayed for the king, the angel of Our Lord appeared to him, and laid a schedule upon the altar, where the sin of the king was written by order and it was pardoned him by the prayers of Saint Giles, so that he were thereof repentant, and abstained him from doing it any more. And it was adjoined at the end that who that required Saint Giles for any sin that he had done, if he left it, that it should be pardoned to him. And after the holy man delivered the schedule to the king, and he confessed his sin and required pardon publicly.

Then Saint Giles returned thence with honour, and when he came to the city of Nismes, he raised the son of a prince that was dead. And a little while after he denounced that his monastery should be destroyed of enemies of the faith. And after he went to Rome and got privileges of the Pope to his church, and two doors of cypress in which were the images of Saint Peter and Paul. And he threw them into the Tiber at Rome, and recommended them to God for to govern. And when he returned to his monastery he made a lame man to go, and found the two doors of cypress at the gate of his monastery. Whereof he thanked God that had kept them without breaking in so many adventures as they had been in, and soon he set them at the gates of the church for the beauty of them, and for the grace that the Church of Rome had done thereto.

And at the last Our Lord shewed to him his departing out of this world, and he said it to his brethren, and admonished them to pray for him, and so he slept and died godly in Our Lord.

And many witness that they heard the company of angels bearing the soul of him in to heaven. And he flourished about the year of Our Lord VII C.

X.—THE LEGEND OF SAINT JULIAN HOSPITATOR.

JULIAN there was that slew his father and mother by innocence. And this man was noble and young, and gladly went for to hunt. And one time among all other he found an hart which returned toward him, and said to him: "Thou huntest me that shalt slay thy father and mother." Hereof was he much abashed and afeard, and for dread that it should happen to him that the hart had said to him, he went privily away that no man knew thereof, and found a prince, noble and great, to whom he put him in service. And he proved so well in battle and in services in his palace, that he was so much in the prince's grace that he made him knight, and gave to him a rich widow of a castellan, and for her dower he received the castle. And when his father and mother knew that he was thus gone, they put them in the way for to seek him in many places. And so long they went till they came to the castle where he dwelled. But then he was gone out, and they found his wife. And when she saw them she enquired diligently who they were. And when they had said and recounted what was happened of their son, she knew verily that they were the father and

mother of her husband, and received them much
charitably, and gave to them her own bed and
made another for herself. And on the morrow
the wife of Julian went to the church, and her
husband came home while she was at the church.
And he entered into his chamber for to awake
his wife. And he saw twain in his bed, and
weened that it had been a man that had lain with
his wife, and slew them both with his sword.
And after he went out and saw his wife coming
from the church. Then was he much abashed,
and demanded of his wife who they were that lay
in his bed. Then she said that they were his
father and his mother which had long sought him,
and she had laid them in his bed. Then he
swooned and was almost dead and began to weep
bitterly and cry: " Alas! caitiff that I am, what
shall I do that have slain my father and mother?
Now it is happened that I supposed to have es-
chewed." And he said to his wife, " Adieu and
farewell, my right dear love. I shall never rest
till that I shall have knowledge if God will pardon
and forgive me this that I have done, and that I
shall have worthy penance therefore." And she
answered: " Right dear love, God forbid that ye
should go without me. Like as I have had joy
with you so will I have pain and heaviness."
Then departed they and went till they came to a
great river over which much folk passed, where
they edified an hospital much great for to harbour
poor people, and there did their penance in bearing men over that would pass.

After long time, Saint Julian slept about midnight sore travailed, and it was frore and much cold. And he heard a voice lamenting and crying, that said : "Julian, come and help us over." And anon he arose and went over and found one almost dead for cold. Anon he took him and bare him to the fire and did great labour to chafe and warm him. And when he saw that he could not be chafed nor warmed, he bare him into his bed and covered him the best wise he might. And anon after he that was so sick and appeared as he had been measle, he saw all shining ascend into heaven. And he said to Saint Julian, his host, "Julian, Our Lord hath sent me to thee and sendeth thee word that He hath accepteth thy penance." And awhile after, Saint Julian and his wife rendered unto God their souls and departed out of this world.

ATHERINE is said of catha, that is, all, and ruin, that is, falling; for all the edifice of the devil fell from her. For the edifice of pride fell from her by humility that she had, and the edifice of fleshly desires fell from her by her virginity, and worldly covetise, for she despised all worldly things. Or Katherine may be said as a little chain; for she made a chain of good works by which she mounted into heaven. And this chain or ladder hath four grees or steps, which be innocence of work, cleanness of body, despising of vanity, and saying of truth. Which the prophet putteth by order when he saith, "Quis ascendet in montem domini? Innocens manibus." "Who shall ascend into the mountain of Our Lord; that is, heaven." And he answereth "The innocent of his hands, he that is clean in his heart, he that hath not taken in vain his soul, and he that hath not sworn in fraud and deceit to his neighbour." And it appeareth in her legend how these four degrees were in her.

Katherine by descent of line was of the noble lineage of the Emperors of Rome. Whose most blessed life and conversation wrote the solemn doctor Anathasius which knew her lineage and her life, for he was one of her masters in her tender age before she was converted to the Christian faith. And after, the said Anathasius by her preaching and marvellous works was converted also, which after her martyrdom was made Bishop of Alexandria and a glorious pillar of the Church by the grace of God and merits of Saint Katherine.

As we find by credible chronicles, in the time of Diocletian and Maximian was great and cruel tyranny shewed in all the world as well to Christian men as to paynims, so that many that were subject to Rome put away the yoke of servage and rebelled openly against the Empire. Among whom the realm of Armenia was one that withstood most the tribute of the Romans. Wherefore they of Rome deputed a noble man of dignity named Constantine which was tofore other a valiant man in arms, discreet and virtuous. The which lord after he came in to Armenia anon subdued them by his discreet prudence and deserved to have the love and favour of his enemies, in so much that he was desired to marry the daughter of the king, which was sole heir of the realm, and he consented and married her. And soon after, the king her father died and then Constantine was enhanced and crowned king, which soon after had a son by his wife named Costus, at the birth of whom his mother died. After the death of whom Constantine returned to Rome to see the Emperor and to know how his lordships were governed. In the meantime tidings came to Rome how that Great Britain which now is called England rebelled against the Empire. Wherefore by the advice of the Consuls, it was concluded that Constantine, King of Armenia, should go into Britain to subdue them, which addressed him thither. And in short time after he entered into the land, by his prowess and wisdom he appeased the realm and subdued it again to the Empire of Rome. And also he was so acceptable to the king of Britain named Coel that he married his daughter Helena, which afterward found the holy cross. And in short time he gat on her Constantine which afterward was Emperor. And then soon after died Constantine, and Constantine after the death of king Coel, by his mother was crowned King of Britain. And Costus the first son of Constantine, wedded the king's daughter of Cyprus which was heir. Of whom, as shall be hereafter said, was engendered Saint Katherine which came of the lineage of Constantine.

In the year of Our Lord two hundred, reigned in Cyprus a noble and prudent king named Costus, which was a noble and seemly man, rich and of good conditions, and had to wife a queen like to himself in virtuous governance. Which lived together prosperously, but after the law of paynims and worshipped idols. This king, because he loved renown and would have his name spread through the world, he founded a city in which he edified a temple of his false gods. And he named that city after his name Costi : which after, to increase his fame, the people named it Fama Costi, and yet unto this day is called Famagusta. In which city he and the queen lived in great wealth and prosperity.

And like as the fair rose springeth among the briars and thorns, right so between these two paynims was brought forth the blessed virgin, Saint Katherine. And when this holy virgin was born, she was so fair of visage and so well formed in her members that all the people enjoyed in her beauty. And when she came to seven years of age, anon after she was set to school; where she profitted much more than any other of her age and was informed in the arts liberal, wherein she drank plenteously of the well of wisdom. For she was chosen to be a teacher and informer of everlasting wisdom.

The king Costus her father had so great joy of the great towardness and wisdom of his daughter, that he let ordain a tower in his palace with divers studies and chambers in which she might be at her pleasures and also at her will. And also be ordained for to wait on her seven the best masters and wisest in cunning that might be gotten in those parts. And within a while they that came to teach her they after learned of her and became her disciples.

And when this virgin came to the age of thirteen years, her father King Costus died and then she was left as queen and heir after him. And then the estates of the land came to this young lady Katherine and desired her to make a parliament, in which she might be crowned and receive the homage of her subjects : and that such rule might be set in her beginning, that peace and prosperity might ensue in her realm. And this young maid granted to them their asking.

And when the parliament was assembled and the young queen crowned with great solemnity, and she sitting on a day in a parliament, and her mother by her with all the lords each in his place, a lord arose, by the assent of her mother, the other lords and commons, and kneeled down before her, saying these words, " Right high and mighty princess and our most sovereign lady, please it you to wit that I am commanded by the queen your mother, by all the lords and commons of this your realm, to require your highness that it may please you to grant to them that they might provide some noble king or prince to marry you, to the end that he might rule and defend your realm and subjects like as your father did before you ; and also that of you might proceed noble lineage which after you might reign upon us. Which thing we most desire and hereof we desire your good answer."

This young queen Katherine hearing this request was abashed and troubled in her courage, how she might answer to content her mother, the lords, and her subjects, and to keep herself chaste. For she had concluded to keep her virginity and rather to suffer death than to defoul it. And then with a sad cheer and meek look she answered in this wise :

"Cousin, I have well understood your request, and thank my mother, the lords, and my subjects of the great love that they all have to me and to my realm. As touching my marriage, I trust verily there may be no peril, considering the great wisdom of my lady my mother and of the lords, with the good obeisance of the commons, trusting in their good continuance. Wherefore we need not to seek a stranger for to rule us and our realm, for with your good assistance and aid we hope to rule, govern, and keep this our realm in good justice, peace, and rest, in like wise as the king my father held you in. Wherefore at this time I pray you to be content and to cease of this matter and let us proceed to such matters as be request for the rule, governance, and universal weal of this realm."

And when this young queen Katherine had achieved her answer, the queen her mother and all the lords were abashed of her words and wist not what to say. For they considered well by her words that she had no will to be married. And then there arose and stood up a duke which was her uncle, and with due reverence, he said unto her in this wise :

"My sovereign lady, saving your high and noble discretion, this answer is full heavy to my lady your mother and to us all your humble liegemen, without you take better advice to your noble courage. Wherefore I shall move to you of four notable things that the great God hath endowed you with before all other creatures that we know. Which things ought to cause you to take a lord to your husband, to the end that the plenteous gifts of nature and grace may spring of you by generation, which may succeed by right line to reign upon us, to the great comfort and joy of all your people and subjects : and the contrary would turn to great sorrow and heaviness." "Now good uncle," said she, "what be these four notable things that so ye repute in us?" "Madame," said he, "the first is this that we be ascertained that ye be come of the most noble blood of all the world. The second, that ye be a great inheritor, and the greatest that liveth of women to our knowledge. The third is, that in science, cunning and wisdom ye pass all other. And the fourth is, in bodily shape and beauty, there is none like to you. Wherefore, madam, us think that these four notable things must needs constrain you to incline to our request."

Then said this young queen Katherine, with a sad countenance, "Now, uncle, since God and nature have wrought so great virtues in us, we be so much more bounden to love and to please Him, and we thank Him humbly of His great and large gifts. But since you desire so much that we should consent to be married, we let you plainly to wit that like as you have described us so will we describe him that we will have to our lord and husband. And if we can get such one we will agree to take him with all our heart. For he that shall be lord of my heart and mine husband shall have these four notable things in him

over all measure; so ferforthly that all creatures
shall have need of him and he need of none.
And he that shall be my lord must be of as
noble blood that all men shall do to him worship: and therewith so great a lord that I shall
never think that I made him a king: and so rich
that he pass all other in riches. And so full of
beauty must he be that all angels have joy to
behold him: and so pure that his mother be a
virgin: and so meek and benign that he can
gladly forgive all offences done to him. Now I
have described to you him that I will have and
desire to my lord and to my husband, go ye and
seek him, and if ye can find such a one, I will be
his wife with all my heart if he vouchsafe to have
me. And finally, but if ye find such a one, I
will never take none. And take this for a final
answer." And with this she cast down her eyes
meekly and held her still.

And when the queen her mother and the lords
heard this, they made great sorrow and heaviness:
for they saw well that there was no remedy in
that matter. Then said her mother to her with an
angry voice. "Alas, daughter, is this your great
wisdom that is talked of so far? Much sorrow
be ye like to do to me and all yours. Alas, who
saw ever woman forge to her such an husband
with such virtues as ye do? For such one as ye
have devised there was never none nor never shall
be. And therefore daughter leave this folly and
do as your noble elders have done tofore you."

And then said this young queen Katharine unto

her mother with a piteous sighing : " Madam, I
wot well by very reason that there is one much
better than I can devise him. And but he by
his grace find me I shall never have joy. For I
feel by great reason that there is a way that we be
clean out of, and we be in darkness and till the
light of grace come we may not see the clear
way. And when it pleaseth him to come, he
shall avoid all darkness of the clouds of ignorance
and shew him clearly to me whom my heart so
fervently desireth and loveth. Wherefore I beseech you meekly my lady mother, that ye nor
none other move me more of this matter. For I
promise you plainly that, for to die therefore, I
shall never have other husband, but only him
that I have described, to whom I shall truly keep
me with all the pure love of mine heart."

And with this she arose and her mother and all
the lords of the parliament with great sorrow and
lamentation, and taking their leave departed.
And this noble young Katherine went to her
palace, whose heart was set a-fire upon this husband that she had devised; so that she could do
no thing but all her mind and intent was set on
him. And she continually mused how she might
find him but she could not find the mean. Howbeit He was nigh to her heart that she sought;
for he had kindled a burning love which could
never after be quenched for no pain nor tribulation, as it appeared in her passion.

But now I leave this young queen in her contemplation and shall say you, as far as God will

give me grace, how that Our Lord by his special miracle called her to baptism in a special manner, such as hath not been heard of before or since, and also how she was visibly married to Our Lord in showing to her sovereign tokens of singular love.

Then beside Alexandria a certain space of miles, dwelled a hermit in the desert named Adrian which had served Our Lord continually by the space of thirty years in great penance. And on a day as he walked before his cell, being in his holy meditations, there came against him the most reverend lady that ever any earthly creature might behold. And when this holy man beheld her high estate and excellent beauty which was above nature, he was sore abashed and so much astonished that he fell down as he had been dead. Then this blessed lady seeing this, called him by his name goodly and said: "Brother Adrian, dread ye no thing for I am come to you for your good honour and profit." And with that she took him up meekly, comforting him, and said in this wise: "Adrian, ye must go on a message for me into the city of Alexandria and in to the palace of the queen Katherine. And say to her that the lady saluteth her whose son she hath chosen to be her lord and husband, sitting in her parliament with her mother and lords about her, where she had a great conflict and battle to keep her virginity. And say to her that this same lord whom she chose is my Son, that am a pure Virgin, and He desireth her beauty and loveth her

E

chastity among all the virgins on the earth. I command her without tarrying that she come with thee alone unto this place, whereas she shall be new clothed, and then shall she see Him and have Him unto her everlasting spouse."

Then Adrian, bearing this, said dreadfully in this wise: "Ah, Blessed Lady how shall I do this message? For I know not the city nor the way thither: and who am I, though I knew it, to do such a message to the queen. For her meinie will not suffer me to come into her presence, and though I came to her she will not believe me but put me in duress as I were a deceiver." "Adrian," said this Blessed Lady, "dread ye not; but go ye forth and ye shall find no letting, and enter into her chamber: For the angel of my Lord shall lead you thither and bring you both hither safely."

Then he, meekly obeying, went forth into Alexandria and entered into the palace. And he found doors and closures opening against him; and so passed from chamber to chamber till he came into her secret study whereas none came but herself alone. And there he found her in her holy contemplation and did to her his message, like as you have heard, according to his charge. And when this blessed virgin Katherine had heard his message and understood by certain tokens that he came for to fetch her to him who she so fervently desired, anon she arose forgetting her estate and meinie. And she followed the old man through her palace and the city of Alexandria, unknown of any person, and so into the desert. In which

way as they walked, she demanded of him many
an high question, and he answered to her sufficiently in all her demands, and informed her in
the faith, and she benignly received his doctrine.

And as they thus went in the desert, this holy
man had lost his way, and wist not where he was.
And he was all confused in himself, and said secretly: "Alas! I fear me I am deceived, and that
this be an illusion. Alas! shall this virgin here
be perished among these wild beasts? Now,
blessed Lady, help me that am almost in despair:
and save this maiden that hath forsaken for your
love all that she had, and hath obeyed your commandment." And as he thus sorrowed, the
blessed virgin Katherine perceived, and she demanded him what ailed him and why he sorrowed.
And he said, "For you: by cause I cannot find
my cell, nor wot not where I am." "Father,"
said she, "dread ye not; for trust ye verily that
that good Lady which sent you for me shall not
suffer us to perish in this wilderness." And then
she said to him, "What monastery is yonder that
I see which is so rich and fair to behold?" And
he demanded of her where she saw it, and she
said, "Yonder, in the East." Then he wiped his
eyes and saw the most glorious monastery that ever
he saw. Whereof he was full of joy, and said to
her: "Now, blessed be God which hath endued
you with so perfect faith. For there is that place
wherein ye shall receive so great worship and joy."
"Now good father Adrian, hie ye fast that we
were there: for therein is all my desire and joy."

And soon after they approached that glorious place. And when they came to the gate, there met them a glorious company all clothed in white and with chaplets of white lilies on their heads. Whose beauty was so great and bright that the virgin Katherine nor the old man might not behold them, but all ravished fell down in great dread. Then one more excellent than another spake unto the virgin Katherine: "Stand up, our dear sister, for ye be right welcome," and led her further in till they came to the second gate. There another more glorious company met her all clothed in purple, with fresh chaplets of red roses on their heads. And the holy vigrin seeing them, fell down for reverence and dread. And they benignly comforting her, took her up and said to her: "Dread ye no thing, our dear sister, for there was never none more heartily welcome to our Sovereign Lord than ye be and to us all. For ye shall receive our clothing and our crown with so great honour that all saints shall joy in you. Come forth for the Lord abideth desiring you." And then this blessed virgin Katherine with trembling joy passed forth with them like as she that was ravished with so marvellous joy that she could not speak. And when she was entered into the body of the church, she heard a melody of marvellous sweetness which passed all hearts to think it. And there they beheld a royal queen standing in her estate with a great multitude of angels and saints, whose beauty and richness might no heart think and no pen write, for it exceedeth

ST. KATHERINE.

every man's mind. Then the noble company of martyrs with the fellowship of virgins which led the virgin Katherine fell down flat before this royal Empress with sovereign reverence, saying in this wise : "Our most Sovereign Lady, Queen of Heaven, Lady of all the World, Empress of Hell, Mother of Almighty God King of Bliss, to whose commandment obey all creatures heavenly and earthly, liketh it you that we here present to you our dear sister, whose name is written in the book of life : beseeching your benign grace to receive her as your daughter chosen and humble hand-maid for to accomplish the work which our Blessed Lord hath begun in her." And with that our Blessed Lady said : "Bring ye me my well-beloved daughter." And when the holy virgin heard our Lady speak, she was so much re-plenished with heavenly joy that she lay as she had been dead.

Then the holy company took her up and brought her tofore our Blessed Lady. Unto whom she said, "My dear daughter, ye be wel-come to me. And be ye strong and of good comfort, for ye be specially chosen of my Son for be honoured. Remember ye not how sitting in your parliament ye described to you an husband, where as ye had a great conflict and battle in de-fending your chastity?" And then this holy Katherine kneeling with humble reverence and dread said, "O most Blessed Lady, blessed be ye among all women. I remember how I chose the lord which then was full far from my knowledge.

But now, Blessed Lady, by His mighty power and your special grace, he hath opened the eyes of my blind conscience so that now I see the clear way of truth. And humbly beseech you most Blessed Lady, that I may have Him Whom my heart loveth and desireth above all things, without Whom I may not live." And with these words her spirits were so fast closed that she lay as she had been dead. And then our Lady in comforting her said, "My dear daughter, it shall be as ye desire. But yet ye lack one thing that ye must receive or ye come to the presence of my Son. Ye must be clothed with the sacrament of baptism. Wherefore come on my dear daughter, for all thing is provided." For there was a font solemnly apparelled with all thing requisite unto baptism.

And then our Blessed Lady called Adrian the old father to her and said, "Brother, this office belongeth to you, for ye be a priest. Therefore baptize ye my daughter. But ye shall not change her name but Katherine shall she be named still. And I shall be her godmother." And then this holy man Adrian baptized her.

And after our Lady said to her, "Now mine own daughter be glad and joyful, for ye lack no thing that belongeth to the wife of an heavenly spouse. And now I shall bring you to my Lord, my Son which abideth for you."

And so our Lady led her forth unto the choir door; whereas she saw our Saviour Jesus Christ with a great multitude of angels, whose beauty is impossible to be thought or written of earthly creature. Of whose sight this blessed virgin was fulfilled with so great sweetness that it cannot be expressed.

Then our Blessed Lady benignly said, "Most sovereign honour, joy and glory be to you, King of Bliss, my Lord, my God and my son. Lo I have brought here unto your blessed presence your humble servant Katherine, which for your love hath refused all earthly things, and hath at my sending obeyed to come hither, hoping and trusting to receive that I promised to her." Then our Blessed Lord took up his mother and said, "Mother that which pleaseth you pleaseth me and your desire is mine, for I desire that she be knit to me by marriage among all the virgins of the earth."

And He said to her, "Katherine come hither to me." And as soon as she heard Him name her name, so great a sweetness entered into her soul that she was as all ravished. And therewith our Lord gave to her a new strength which passed nature, and said to her, "Come my spouse and give to me your hand." And there our Lord espoused her in joining Himself to her in spiritual marriage promising ever to keep her in all her life in this world and after this life to reign perpetually in His bliss. And in token of this He set a ring on her finger which He commanded her to keep in remembrance of this, and said, "Dread ye not my dear spouse. I shall not depart from you but alway comfort and strengthen you."

Then said this new espouse, "O Blessed Lord, I thank you with all mine heart of all your great mercies: beseeching you, Sovereign Lord, to make me digne and worthy to be Thy servant and handmaid and to please you whom my heart loveth and desireth above all things."

And then this glorious marriage was made, whereof all the celestial court joyed and sang this verse in heaven.

Sponsus amat sponsam
Salvator visitat illam ;

with so great melody that no heart may express ne think it. This was a glorious and singular marriage, to which was never none like before on earth. Wherefore this virgin Katherine ought to be honoured, lauded and praised among all virgins that ever were in earth. And then our Blessed Lord after this marriage said unto the blessed Katherine "Now the time is come that I must depart unto the place that I came from, wherefore what that ye will desire I am ready to grant to you. And after My departing ye must abide here with old Adrian ten days till ye be perfectly informed in all My laws and will. And when ye shall become home, ye shall find your mother dead. But dread ye not: for ye were never missed there in all this time. For I ordained there one in your stead and all men ween it is yourself. And when ye come home, she that is there in your stead shall void. Now farewell, my dear spouse." And then she cried with a full piteous voice "Ah, my sovereign Lord God and

all the joy of my soul, have ever mind on me."
And with that He blessed her and vanished away
from her sight.

And then for sorrow of His departing, she fell
in a swoon so that she lay still a large hour without any life. And then was Adrian a sorry man
and cried upon her so long that at the last she
came to herself, and revived, and lift up her eyes
and saw nothing about her save an old cell and
the old man Adrian by her weeping. For all the
royalty was voided both the monastery and palace
and all the comfortable sights that she had seen:
specially He which was cause of all her joy and
comfort. And then she sorrowed mourned and
wept, unto the time that she saw the ring on her
finger. And for joy thereof she swooned; and
after, she kissed it a thousand times with many a
piteous tear. And then Adrian comforted her
the best wise he could with many a blessed ex-
hortation; and the blessed virgin Katherine took
all his comforts and obeyed him as to her father.
And she dwelled with him the time that our
Lord had assigned her, till she was sufficiently
taught in all that was needful to her. And then
she went home to her palace, and governed her
holily in converting many creatures to the faith
of Jesus Christ, on Whom all her joy was wholly
set and ever He was in her mind, and so dwelled
still in her palace, never idle, but ever in the service of Our Lord, full of charity. Where awhile
I let her dwell fulfilled of virtues and grace.

And then in the meantime Maxentius that was

then Emperor and vicious to God's law and a cruel tyrant considered the noble and royal city of Alexandria and came thither and assembled all the people, rich and poor, for to make sacrifice to the idols. And the Christian men that would not make sacrifice he let slay. And this holy virgin was at that time eighteen years of age, dwelling in her palace full of riches and of servants, alone without parents and kin. And she heard the braying and noise of beasts and the joy that they made and song and marvelled what it might be, and sent one of her servants hastily to inquire what it was. And when she knew it, she took some of the people of her palace, and garnished her with the sign of the cross, and went thither and found there many Christian men to be led to do sacrifice for fear of death.

Then was she strongly troubled for sorrow, and went forth hardily to the emperor and said in this wise : " The dignity of thine order and the way of reason have moved me to salute thee, if it may be that thou canst know the Creator and Maker of heaven, and wouldst revoke thy courage from worshipping of false gods." And then she disputed of many things with Cæsar tofore the gates of the temple. And then she began to say :

" I have set my cure to say these things to thee as to a wise man. Wherefore hast thou now assembled this multitude of people thus in vain for to adore the folly of the idols ? Hast thou marvel of this temple that is made with man's hand ? Wonderest thou on the precious ornaments which be as dust tofore the wind ? Thou shouldst rather marvel thee of heaven and of the earth and of all the things that be therein, and of the sun, the moon, the stars and planets that have been since the beginning of the world, and shall be as long as it shall please God. And marvel thee of the ornaments of heaven, that is to say, the sun, moon, stars and planets how they move from the orient into the occident and never be weary. And when thou shalt have knowledge of all these things and hast apperceived it, demand after who is most mighty of all. And when thou knowest Him that is Sovereign and Maker of all things, to Whom none is semblable nor like, then adore Him and glorify, for He is God of gods and Lord of lords."

And when she had disputed of many things of the Incarnation of the Son of God much wisely, the Emperor was much abashed and could not answer to her. But at the last, when he was come to himself, he said to her, " O thou woman, suffer us to finish our sacrifice, and after we shall give to thee an answer." Then commanded he that she should be led to his palace and be kept with great diligence, and marvelled much of her great prudence and of her great beauty. For she was right fair to behold unto all the people.

And when the Emperor saw that in no manner he could resist her wisdom, he sent secretly by letter for all the great grammarians and rhetoricians that they should come hastily to his prætory at Alexandria, and he should give to them great gifts if they might surmount a maiden well bespoken. And there were then brought from divers provinces fifty masters which surmounted all mortal men in worldly wisdom. And then demanded they for what cause they were called from so far parts. And the Emperor answered and said, "We have a maiden, none comparable to her in wit and wisdom, which confoundeth all wise men, and she saith that our gods be devils. And if ye surmount her by honour, I shall send you again to your countries with joy." And one of them had hereof despite and said by disdain, "This is a worthy counsel of an Emperor that for one maid young and frail, he hath done assembled so many sages and from so far countries, and one of our clerks or scholars may overcome her." And the king said to them, "I may well by strength constrain her to do sacrifice but I had liefer that she were overcome by your arguments." Then said they, "Let her be brought tofore us and when she shall be overcome in her folly, she may know that she never saw wise men till now."

And when the virgin knew the strife of the disputation that she abode, she commended herself all unto Our Lord. And when she was brought tofore the masters and orators, she said to the Emperor, "What judgment is this to set fifty orators and masters against one maid, and to promise to them great rewards for their victory: and thou compellest me to dispute with them without hope of any reward? Jesus Christ which is very guerdon of them that strive for Him shall be only with me and He shall be my reward.

And when the virgin had right wisely disputed and that she had confounded their gods by open reasons, they were abashed and wist not what to say but were all still. And the Emperor was replenished with felony against them, and began to blame them by cause they were overcome so foully of one maid. And then one that was master above all the other, said to the Emperor, "Know thou, sir Emperor, that never was there any that might stand against us but that anon he was overcome. But this maid hath so converted us that we cannot say anything against Jesus Christ, ne we may not ne dare not. Wherefore, sir Emperor, we knowledge that but if thou mayest bring forth a more proveable sentence concerning them that we have worshipped hitherto, that all we be converted to Jesus Christ."

And when the tyrant heard this thing, he was esprised with great woodness, and commanded that they all should be burnt in the midst of the city. And the holy virgin comforted them and made them constant to martyrdom and informed them diligently in the faith. And because they doubted that they should die without baptism, the virgin said to them: "Doubt ye no thing. For the effusion of your blood shall be reputed to you for baptism. And garnish you with the sign of the cross and ye shall be crowned in heaven." And when they were cast in to the flames of fire, they rendered their souls unto God, and neither hair nor cloth of them had none harm nor was hurt by the fire.

And when the Christian men had buried them, the tyrant spake unto the virgin and said : "Right noble lady virgin, have pity of thy youth and thou shalt be chief of my palace next the queen. And thine image shall be set up in the midst of of the city and shall be adored of all the people as a goddess." To whom the virgin said : "Leave to say such things, for it is evil to think it. I am given and married to Jesus Christ, He is my spouse, He is my glory, He is my love, He is my sweetness. There may no fair words nor no torments call me from Him." Then he being full of woodness commanded that she should be despoiled naked and beaten with scorpions and so beaten to be put in a dark prison and there to be tormented by hunger for the space of twelve days.

And the emperor went out of the country for certain causes. And the queen was taken with great love of the virgin and went by night to the prison with Porphyry, the prince of knights. And when the queen entered, she saw the prison shining by great clearness and angels anointing the wounds of the holy virgin Katherine. And then Saint Katherine began to preach to the queen the joys of paradise, and converted her to the Christian faith, and said to her that she should receive the crown of martyrdom. And thus spake they together till midnight. And when. Porphyry had heard all that she had said, he fell down to her feet and received the faith of Jesus

Christ with two hundred knights. And because the tyrant had commanded that she should be twelve days without meat and drink, Jesus Christ sent to her a white dove which fed her with celestial meat. And after this, Jesus Christ appeared to her with a great multitude of angels and virgins, and said to her: "Daughter, know thy Maker for whom thou hast enterprized this travailous battle. Be thou constant for I am with thee."

And when the emperor was returned, he commanded that she should be brought to him. And when he saw her so shining whom he supposed to her been tormented by great famine and fasting, he supposed that some had fed her in the prison, and was fulfilled with fury and commanded to torment the keepers of the prison. And she said to him: "Verily, I took never since meat of man; but Jesus Christ had fed me by his angel."

"I pray thee," said the emperor, "set at thine heart this that I do admonish thee and answer not by doubtful words. We will not hold thee as a chamberer but thou shalt triumph as a queen in my realm in beauty enhanced." To whom the blessed virgin said: "Understand I pray thee and judge truly. Whom ought I better to choose of these two? Or the king puissant, perdurable, glorious and fair or one sick, unsteadfast, not noble and foul." And then the emperor having disdain, and angry by felony said: "Of these two choose the one: or do sacrifice and live, or suffer divers torments and perish." And she said "Tarry not to do what torments thou wilt. For

I desire to offer to God my blood and my flesh like as He offered for me. He is my God, my Father, my Friend and my only Spouse."

And then a master warned and advised the king, being wood for anger, that he should make four wheels of iron environed with sharp razors cutting, so that she might be horribly detrenched and cut in that torment, that he might fear the other Christian people by example of that cruel torment. And then was ordained that two wheels should turn against the other two by great force so that they should break all that should be between. And then the blessed virgin prayed Our Lord that He would break these engines to the praising of His name and for to convert the people that were there. And anon, as this blessed virgin was set in this torment, the angel of Our Lord brake the wheels by so great force that it slew four thousand paynims.

And the queen that beheld these things and had hid her faith till then, descended anon and began to blame the Emperor for so great cruelty. And then the king was replenished with woodness when he saw that the queen despised to do sacrifice, and first did do rent off her paps and after smite off her head. And as she was led to martyrdom, she prayed Katherine to pray God for her. And she said to her: "Ne doubt thee nothing, well beloved of God, for this day thou shalt have the realm perdurable for this transitory realm, and an immortal spouse for a mortal." And she was constant and firm in the faith, and bade the tormentors do as was to them commanded. And then the sergeants brought her out of the city and rased off her paps with tongues of iron and after smote off her head.

And Porphyry took away her body and buried it. The next day following was demanded where the body of the queen was. And the Emperor bade that many should be put to torment for to know where the body was. Porphyry came then tofore them all and cried aloud saying " I am he that buried the body of the ancil and servant of Jesus Christ, and have received the faith of God." And then Maxentius began to roar and bray as a mad man and cried, saying : " O wretched and caitiff : Lo, Porphyry, which was the only keeper of my soul and comfort of all mine evils, is deceived." Which thing he told to his knights. To whom they said : " And we also be Christian, and be ready to suffer for Jesus Christ." And then the Emperor, drunken in woodness, commanded that all should be beheaded, and that their bodies should be cast to dogs.

And then he called Katherine and said to her : " How be it that thou hast made the queen to die by thine art magic, if thou repent thee, thou shalt be first and chief in my palace. For thou shalt this day do sacrifice, or thou shalt lose thine head." And she said to him : " Do all that thou hast thought, I am ready to suffer all." And then he gave sentence against her and commanded to smite off her head.

And when she was brought to the place ordained thereto, she lift up her eyes to heaven, praying, and said : "O Jesus Christ, hope and help of them that believe in Thee, O beauty and glory of virgins, good king, I beseech and pray Thee that who somever shall remember my passion, be it at his death or in any other necessity, and shall call me, that he may have by Thy mercy the effect of his request and prayer." And then came a voice to her, saying : "Come unto me my fair love and my spouse ; lo, behold the gate of heaven is open to thee. And also to them that shall hallow thy passion, I promise the comfort of heaven of that they require."

And when she was beheaded, there issued out of her body milk instead of blood, and angels took the body and bare it unto the Mount of Sinai, more than twenty journeys from thence, and buried it there honourably : and continually oil runneth out of her bones which healeth all maladies and sickness. And she suffered death under Maxentius the tyrant, about the year of Our Lord three hundred.

XII.—THE LEGEND OF SAINT MARGARET.

ARGARET is said of a precious gem or ouch that is named a margarite (pearl) which gem is white, little and virtuous. So the blessed Margaret was white by virginity, little by humility, and virtuous by operation of miracles. The virtue of this stone is said to be against effusion of blood, against passion of the heart and to comforting of the spirit. In like wise, the blessed Margaret had virtue against shedding of her blood by constancy, for in her martyrdom she was most constant : and also against the passion of the heart, that is to say, temptation of the devil for she overcame the devil by victory : and to the comforting of the spirit by doctrine, for by her doctrine she converted much people. Theotinus a learned man wrote her legend.

The holy saint Margaret was of the city of Antioch, daughter of Theodosius, patriarch of the idols of paynims. And she was delivered to a nurse for to be kept. And when she came to a perfect age she was baptized, wherefore she was was in great hate of her father.

On a certain day when she was fifteen years of

age, and kept the sheep of her nurse with other maidens, the provost Olybrius passed by the way whereas she was and considered in her so great beauty and fairness that anon he burned in her love and sent his servants and bade them take her and bring her to him. "For if she be free, I shall take her unto my wife and if she be bond I shall make her my concubine."

And when she was presented tofore him, he demanded her of her lineage name and religion. And she answered that she was of noble lineage and her name Margaret and Christian in religion. To whom the provost said, "The two first things be convenient to thee, that is that thou art noble and art ca led Margaret which is a most fair name. But the third appertaineth nothing to thee that so fair a maid and so noble should worship a God crucified." To whom she said, "How knowest thou that Christ was crucified? He answered, "By the books of Christian men." To whom Margaret said, "O what shame it is to you when ye read the pain of Christ and the glory and believe one thing and deny the other." And she said and affirmed Him to be crucified by His will for our redemption and now liveth ever in bliss. And then the provost being wroth commanded her to be put in prison.

And the next day following, he commanded that she should be brought to him and then said to her, "O good maid have pity on thy beauty and worship our gods that it may be well." To whom she said, "I worship Him that maketh the earth to tremble, whom the sea dreadeth, and the winds and the creatures obey." To whom the provost said, "But if thou consent to me, I shall make thy body to be all to torn." Then Saint Margaret said "Christ gave Himself over to the death for me, and I desire gladly to die for Christ." Then the provost commanded her to be hanged on an instrument to be tormented of the people, and to be cruelly first beaten with rods and then with iron combs to rent, in somuch that the blood ran out of her body, like as a stream runneth out of a first springing well. They that were there wept and said, "O Margaret verily we be sorry for thee, which see thy body so foul and cruelly torn and rent. O how thy most beauty hast thou lost for thine incredulity and misbelief. Now believe and thou shalt live." The provost covered his face with his mantle for he might not see so much effusion of blood and then commanded that she should be taken down and to shut her in fast prison.

And there was seen a marvellous brightness in the prison by the keepers. And whiles she was in prison she prayed her Lord that he would visibly shew unto her the fiend that had fought with her. And there appeared an horrible dragon and assailed her and would have devoured her. But she made the sign of the cross and anon he vanished away. In another place it is said that he swallowed her in his belly, she making the sign of the cross, and the belly brake asunder and so she issued out all whole and sound. This swallowing and breaking of the belly of the dragon is said that it is apocryphal.†

After this the devil appeared to her in likeness of a man for to deceive her. And when she saw him she went to prayer. And after she arose and the fiend came to her and took her by the hand and said, "That which thou hast done sufficeth to thee; but now cease as to my person." She caught him by the head and threw him to the ground and set her right foot on his neck, saying, "Lie still thou fiend under the foot of a woman." The devil then cried, "O blessed Margaret, I am overcome. If a young man had overcome me I had not recked, but alas I am overcome of a tender virgin, wherefore I make the more sorrow."

Then she constrained that fiend to tell why he came to her. And he answered that he came to her to counsel her for to obey the desire and request of the provost. Then she constrained him to say wherefore he tempted so much and so oft Christian people. To whom he answered that naturally he hated virtuous men. "And though we be oft put aback from them, yet our desire is much to exclude them from the felicity that we have fell from. For we may never obtain nor recover our bliss that we have lost."

And then she demanded what he was. And

† Then came there out of a corner a great horrible dragon and yawned on her so that his mouth was on her head and his tongue was down to her heel, and would have swallowed. And when he had her all in his mouth, he all to burst in sunder for the cross that Margaret made in the entry."—*Liber Festivalis* (a book of sermons founded on the Golden Legend).

he answered, "I am named Veltis, one of them whom Solomon closed in a vessel of brass. And after his death it happed that they of Babylon found this vessel and supposed to have founden great treasure therein. And they brake the vessel and then a great multitude of us devils flew out and filled full the air, alway awaiting and espying where we may assail rightful men." And when he had said thus, she took off her foot and said to him "Flee hence, thou wretched fiend." And anon the earth opened and the fiend sank in.

Then the next day following when the all people were assembled, she was presented tofore the judge. And she not doing sacrifice to the idols was cast into the fire and her body broiled with burning brands, in such wise that all the people marvelled that so tender a maid might suffer so many torments. And after that they put her fast bounden in a great vessel full of water that by changing of the torments the sorrow and feeling of the pain might be the more. But suddenly the earth trembled, and the blessed virgin without any hurt issued out of the water, saying to Our Lord, "I beseech thee, My Lord, that this water may be to me the fount of baptism in to everlasting life." And anon there was heard great thunder, and a dove descended from heaven, and set a golden crown on her head. Then five thousand men believed on Our Lord, and for Christ's love they all were beheaded by the commandment of the provost Olybrius. Then Olybrius seeing the faith of the holy Margaret immoveable, and also fearing that others should be converted to the Christian faith by her gave sentence and commanded that she should be beheaded.

Then she prayed to one Malchus that should behead her that she might have space to pray. And that gotten, she prayed to Our Lord, saying, " Father Almighty, I yield to thee thankings that Thou hast suffered me to come to this glory, beseeching Thee to pardon them that pursue me. And I beseech Thee, good Lord, of thine abundant grace, Thou wilt grant unto all them that write my passion, read it, or hear, and to them that remember me, that they may deserve to have plain remission and forgiveness of all their sins. And also, good Lord, if any woman with child travailing call on me, that Thou wilt keep her from peril and that the child may be delivered without any hurt." And when she had finished her prayer, there was a voice heard from heaven saying that her prayers were heard and granted, and that the gates of heaven were open and abode for her; and bade her come into the country of everlasting rest. Then she, thanking Our Lord, rose up, and bade the hangman accomplish the commandment of the provost. To whom the hangman said, " God forbid that I should slay the virgin of Christ." To whom she said, "If thou do it not thou mayest have no part with me." Then he being afeard and trembling smote off her head, and falling down at her feet gave up the ghost.

Then Theotinus took up the holy body, and bare it into Antioch and buried it in the house of a noble woman and widow named Synclecia. And thus this blessed and holy virgin, Saint Margaret suffered death and received the crown of martyrdom the xiiith kalends of August, as is found in her story : and it is read in another place that it was the iii ides of July.

XIII.—THE LEGEND OF SAINT SYLVESTER.

YLVESTER was son of one Justa and was learned and taught of a priest named Cyrinus, which did marvellously great alms and made hospitalities. It happened that he received a Christian man into his house named Timothy, whom no man would receive for the persecution of tyrants. Now the said Timothy suffered death and passion after a year whiles he preached justly the faith of Christ. It was so that the prefect Tarquinus supposed that Timothy had had great plenty of riches, which he demanded of Saint Sylvester, threatening him to the death but if he delivered them to him. And when he found certainly that Timothy had no great riches, he commanded to Saint Sylvester to made sacrifice to the idols, and if he did not he would make him suffer divers torments. Saint Sylvester answered : " False evil man, thou shalt die this night and shalt have torments that ever shall endure, and shalt know whether thou wilt or not that He whom we worship is very God." Then Saint Sylvester was put in prison and the provost went to dinner. Now it happed that, as he ate, a bone of a fish turned in his throat and stuck fast so that he could neither have it down nor up; and at midnight he died like as Saint Sylvester had said. And then Saint Sylvester was delivered out of prison.

He was so gracious that all Christian men and paynims loved him. For he was fair like an angel to look on, a fair speaker, whole of body, holy in work, good in counsel, patient and charitable, and firmly established in the faith. He had in writing the names of all the widows and orphans that were poor and to them he administered their necessity. He had a custom to fast all Fridays and Saturdays. Now it was so that Melchiades the bishop of Rome died and all the people chose Sylvester for to be the high bishop of Rome: which sore against his will was made Pope. He instituted for to be fasted Wednesday, Friday and Saturday, and the Thursday for to be hallowed as Sunday.

Now it happed the Emperor Constantine did do slay all the Christian men all about where he could find them. And for this cause Saint Sylvester fled out of the town with his clerks and hid him in a mountain. And for the cruelty of Constantine God sent him such a sickness that he became lazar and measle. And by the counsel of his physicians he gat three thousand young children for to have cut their throats to have the blood in a bath all hot, that thereby he might be healed of his measlry. And when he should ascend into his chariot for to go to the place where he should be bathed, the mothers of the children came cry-

ing and praying for sorrow of their children.
And when he understood that they were mothers
of the children, he had great pity on them, and
said to his knights and them that were about him :
" The dignity of the Empire of Rome is brought
forth of the fountain of pity, the which hath
stablished by decree that who that slayeth a child
in battle shall have his head smitten off. Then
should it be great cruelty to us for to do to ours
such things as we defend to strange nations, for
so should cruelty surmount us. It is better that
we leave cruelty and that pity surmount us, and
therefore me seemeth better to save the lives of
these innocents than that by their death I should
have again my health, of which we be not yet
certain. We may recover nothing for to slay
them. For if so were that I should thereby have
health, that should be a cruel health that should
be bought with the death of so many innocents."
Then he commanded to render and deliver again
to the mothers their children ; and gave to each
of them a good gift. And thus made them to
return to their houses with great joy from whence
they departed with great sorrow. And he himself returned again in his chariot unto his palace.

Now it happed that the next night after,
Saint Peter and Saint Paul appeared to this Emperor Constantine, saying unto him, " Because
that thou hast had horror to shed and spill the
blood of innocents, Our Lord Jesus Christ hath
had pity on thee ; and commandeth thee to send
unto such a mountain where Sylvester is hid

with his clerks. And say to him that thou comest for to be baptized of him and thou shalt be
healed of thy malady." And when he was
awaked, he did do call his knights, and commanded them to go to that mountain and bring
the Pope Sylvester to him courteously and fair,
for to speak with him.

When Saint Sylvester saw from far the knights
come to him, he supposed that they sought him
for to be martyred and began to say to his clerks
that they should be firm and stable in the faith
for to suffer martyrdom. When the knights
came to him, they said to him much courteously
that Constantine sent for him and prayed him
that he would come and speak with him. And
forthwith he came.

And when they had inter-saluted each other,
Constantine told to him his vision. And when
Sylvester demanded of him what men they were
that so appeared to him, the Emperor wist not
ne could not name them. Saint Sylvester opened
a book wherein the images of Saint Peter and
Saint Paul were portrayed, and demanded of him
if they were like unto them. Then Constantine
anon knew them and said that he had seen them
in his sleep. Then Saint Sylvester preached to
him the faith of Jesus Christ, and baptized him;
and when he was baptized he was healed forthwith of his measlry.

And then he ordained vii. laws unto holy
church. The first was that all the city should
worship Christ as very God. The second thing

was that whosoever should say any villainy of
Jesus Christ he should be punished.   The third,
whosoever should do villainy to Christian men he
should lose half his goods.   The fourth that the
Bishop of Rome should be chief of all holy
church, like as the Emperor is chief of all the
world.   The fifth, that who that had done or
should do trespass and fled to the church, that he
should be kept there free from all injuries.   The
sixth, that no man should edify any churches
without licence of holy church and consent of
the bishop.   The seventh, that the dime and
tenth part of the possessions should be given to
the church.

After this the Emperor came to Saint Peter's
church and confessed meekly his sins tofore all
the people, and what wrong he had done to
Christian men : and made to dig and cast out
to make the foundations for churches and bare on
his shoulders twelve hods or baskets full of earth.

When Helena the mother of Constantine,
dwelling in Bethany, heard say that the emperor
was become Christian, she sent to him a letter in
which she praised much her son of this that he
had renounced the false idols, but she blamed
him much that he had renounced the law of the
Jews and worshipped a man crucified.   Then Constantine remanded to his mother that she should
assemble the greatest masters of the Jews and
he should assemble the greatest masters of the
Christian men, to the end that they might dispute,
and know which was the truest law.

Then Helena assembled twelve masters which she brought with her, which were the wisest that they might find in that law. And Saint Sylvester and his clerks were of the other party. Then the emperor ordained two paynims, gentiles, for to be their judges, of whom one was named Crato and the other Zenophilus which were proved wise and expert: and they to give the sentence and be judges of the disputation.

Then began one of the masters of the Jews for to maintain and dispute his law. And Saint Sylvester and his clerks answered to his disputation and to them all alway concluding them by Scripture. The judges, which were true and just, held more of the party of Saint Sylvester than of the Jews. Then said one of the masters of the Jews named Zambri, "I marvel," said he, "that ye be so wise and yet incline you to their words. Let us leave all these words and go we to the effect of the deeds." Then he did do come a cruel bull and said a word in his ear, and anon the bull died: then the people were all against Sylvester. Then said Sylvester, "Believe not thou that he hath named in the ear the name of Jesus Christ, but the name of some devil. Know ye verily, it is no great strength to slay a bull, for a man or a lion or a serpent may well slay him. But it is great virtue to raise him again to life. Then if he may not raise him it is by the devil and if he may raise him again to life I shall believe that he is dead by the power of God." And when the judges heard this, they said to

Zambri that had slain the bull that he should raise him again. Then he answered that if Sylzester might raise him in the name of Jesus of Galilee his Master, then he would believe in him. And thereto bound them all the Jews that were there. And Saint Sylvester first made his orisons and prayer to Our Lord, and then came to the bull and said to him in his ear, "Thou cursed creature that art entered into this bull and hast slain him, go out in the name of Jesus Christ. In whose name I command thee, bull, arise thou up and go with the other beasts debonairly." And anon the bull arose and went forth softly. Then the queen and the judges which were paynims were converted to the faith.

In this time it happed that there was at Rome a dragon in a pit, which every day slew with his breath more than three hundred men. Then came the bishops of the idols to the Emperor and said to him : "O thou most holy Emperor, since the time that thou hast received Christian faith, the dragon which is in yonder foss or pit slayeth every day with his breath more than three hundred men." Then sent the Emperor for Saint Sylvester and asked counsel of him of this matter. Saint Sylvester answered that by the might of God he promised to make him cease of this hurt and grief of the people.

Then Saint Sylvester put himself to prayer, and Saint Peter appeared to him and said : "Go surely to the dragon, and the two priests that be with thee take in thy company. And when thou shalt come to him, thou shalt say to him in this manner, 'Our Lord Jesus Christ, which was born of the Virgin Mary, crucified, buried, and arose, and now sitteth on the right hand of the Father, this is He that shall come to doom and judge the living and the dead. I command thee, Satanas, that thou abide Him in this place till He come.' Then thou shalt bind his mouth with a thread and seal it with the seal wherein is the print of the cross. Then thou and the two priests shall come to me whole and safe."

Thus as Saint Peter had said, Saint Sylvester did. And when Saint Sylvester came to the pit, he descended down an hundred and fifty steps, bearing with him two lanterns, and found the dragon. And he said the words that Saint Peter had said to him, and bound his mouth with the thread and sealed it, and afterwards returned. And as he came upward again, he met with two enchanters which followed him for to see if he descended, which were almost dead of the stink of the horrible dragon. Whom he brought with him whole and sound which anon were baptized and a great multitude of people with them.

Thus was the city of Rome delivered from double death, that was from the culture and worshipping of false idols and from the venom of the dragon.

At the last when Saint Sylvester approached toward his death, he called to him the clergy, and admonished them to have charity, and that they should diligently govern their churches, and keep their flock from the wolves.   And after, the year of the Incarnation of Our Lord three hundred and twenty, he departed out of this world and slept in Our Lord.

XIV.—THE PASSION OF THE ELEVEN THOUSAND VIRGINS.

HE Passion of the eleven thousand Virgins was hallowed in this manner.

In Britain was a Christain kin, named Notus or Maurus, which engendered a daughter named Ursula. This daughter shone full of marvellou honesty, wisdom, and beauty, and her fame and renown was borne all about. And the king of England which then was right mighty and subdued many nations to his empire heard the renown of her, and said that he should be well happy if this virgin might be coupled to his son by marriage. And the young man had great desire and will to have her. And there was a solemn embassade sent to the father of Ursula which promised great promises and said many fair words for to have her, and also made many menaces if they returned vainly to their lord.

And then the king of Britain began to be much anguished because that she that was ennobled in the faith of Jesus Christ should be wedded to him that adored idols: because that he wist well she would not consent in no manner, and also because he doubted much the cruelty of the king.

F

And she that was divinely inspired, did so much to her father that she consented to the marriage by such a condition, that for to solace her, he should send to her father ten virgins, and to herself and to those ten other virgins he should send to each a thousand virgins, and should give to her space of three years for to dedicate her virginity; and the young man should be baptized and in those three years he should be informed in the faith sufficiently. And this she did so that by wise counsel, and by virtue of the condition made, he should with draw from his courage.

But this youngling received this condition gladly, and hasted his father, and was baptized, and commanded that all that Ursula had required should be done. And the father of the virgin ordained for his daughter whom he most loved and the others that had need of comfort of men and service, in their company good men for to serve them.

Then virgins came from all parts and men came for to see this great company. And many bishops came for to go with them in their pilgrimage, among whom was Pantulus, bishop of Basle, which went with them to Rome and returned from thence with them and received martyrdom. Saint Gerasina, queen of Sicily, which had made of her husband that was a cruel tyrant a meek lamb, was sister of Matrisius the bishop and of Daria mother of Saint Ursula, to whom the father of Saint Ursula had signified the journey by secret letters. She put herself in the way with her four daughters, Babilla, Juliana, Victoria, and Aura and her little son Adrian, which for the love of his sisters went in the same pilgrimage. And by the counsel of this queen the virgins were gathered together from divers realms and she was leader of them and at the last she suffered martyrdom with them.

And then all things were made ready. Then the queen shewed her counsel to the knights of her company and made them all to swear this new chivalry. And then began they to make divers plays and games of battle and feigned many manner of plays : and for all that they left not their purpose : and sometime they returned from this play at mid-day and sometime unneth at even-song-time. And the barons and the great lords assembled them to see the fair games and disports, and all had joy and pleasure in beholding them and also marvel.

And at the last when Ursula had converted all these virgins unto the faith of Christ, they went all to the sea. And in the space of a day, they sailed over the sea, having so good wind that they arrived at a port of Gaul named Tiel. And from thence came to Cologne ; where an angel of Our Lord appeared to Ursula and told her that they should return again the whole number to that place and there receive the crown of martyrdom. And from thence by monition of the angel they went toward Rome. And when they came to Basle they left there their ships and went to Rome a foot. At the coming of whom the pope

Cyriacus was much glad because he was born in Britain and had many cousins among them. And he with his clerks received them with all honour.

And that same night it was shewed to the pope that he should receive with them the crown of martyrdom, which thing he hid in himself. And he baptized many of them that were not then baptized. And when he saw time convenable, when he had governed the church one year and eleven weeks, and was the nineteenth pope after Saint Peter, he purposed tofore all the people and shewed them his purpose and resigned his office and his dignity. But all men gainsaid it and specially the cardinals, which supposed that he trespassed, leaving the glory of his papacy and would go after these foolish virgins. But he would not agree to abide but ordained an holy man to occupy his place, which was named Ametos. And because he left the siege apostolic against the will of the clergy, the clerks put out his name of the catalogue of popes. And all the grace that he had gotten in his time, this holy company of women made him leave it.

And then two felon princes of the chivalry of Rome, Maximian and Africanus, saw this great company of virgins and that many men and women assembled to them, and doubted that the Christian religion should be much increased by them. Wherefore they enquired diligently of their viage and then sent they messengers to Julian, their cousin, prince of the lineage of the Huns, that he should bring his host against them, and should assemble at Cologne and there behead them because they were Christian.

And the blessed Cyriacus issued out of the city of Rome with this blessed company of virgins : and there followed him Vincent priest cardinal, and James that was come from Britain into Antioch and had holden there seven years the dignity of the bishop, which then had visited the Pope, and was gone out of his city, and held company with these virgins when he heard of their coming and suffered martyrdom with them. And Maurice, bishop of Modena, uncle of Babilla and Juliana, and Solarius, bishop of Lucca with Simplicius, bishop of Ravenna, which then were come to Rome, put them in the company of these virgins.

Now Ethereus the husband of Ursula, abiding in Britain was warned of Our Lord by a vision of an angel that he should exhort his mother to be Christian. For his father died the first year that he was christened and Ethereus his son succeeded after him in his reign. And then when these holy virgins returned from Rome with the bishops, Ethereus was warned of Our Lord that he should anon arise and go to meet his wife at Cologne and there receive with her the crown of martyrdom. Which anon obeyed the admonishments divine and did do baptize his mother. And he came with her and his little sister Florence then also baptized, and with the bishop Clement, meeting the holy virgins and accompanying them unto martyrdom. And Marculus bishop of

Greece and his niece Constantia daughter of Dorotheus king of Constantinople, which was married to the son of a king but he died tofore the wedding and she avowed to Our Lord her virginity, they were also warned by a vision and came to Rome and joined them to these virgins unto the martyrdom.

And then all these virgins came with the bishops to Cologne and found that it was beseiged with the Huns. And when the Huns saw them they began to run upon them with a great cry and a-raged like wolves on sheep and slew all this great multitude. And when they were all be-headed, they came to the blessed Ursula. And the prince of them, seeing her beauty so marvel-lous was abashed : and he began to comfort her upon the death of the virgins and promised her to take her to his wife. And when she had re-fused him and despised him altogether, he shot at her an arrow and pierced her through the body and so accomplished her martyrdom. These vir-gins suffered death the year of Our Lord two hundred and thirty-eight. But some hold opinion that they suffered not death in that time. For Sicily and Constantinople were then no realms. But it is supposed that they suffered death long time afterwards, when the Huns and Goths en-forced them against Christian men in the time of the Emperor Marcian that reigned in the year of Our Lord, four hundred and fifty-nine.

HE Seven Sleepers were born in the city of Ephesus. When Decius the Emperor came into Ephesus for the persecution of Christian men, he commanded to edify the temples in the middle of the city, so that all should come with him to do sacrifice to the idols; and did do seek all the Christian people and bind them for to make them to do sacrifice, or else to put them to death: in such wise, that every man was afraid of the pains that he promised, that the friend forsook his friend, and the son denied his father, and the father the son. And then in this city were founden seven Christian men, that is to wit, Maximian, Malchus, Martian, Dionysius, John, Serapion and Constantine. And when they saw this they had much sorrow: and by cause they were the first in the palace that despised the sacrifices, they hid them in their houses and were in fasting and in prayers. And then they were accused tofore Decius and came thither and were found very Christian men. Then was given to them space for to repent them unto the coming again of Decius. And in the mean while they despended their patrimony in alms to the poor people. And they assembled

themselves together and took counsel and went to
the Mount of Caelion and there ordained to be
more secretly, and there hid them long time.
And one of them administered and served them
alway. And when he went into the city he
clothed him in the habit of a beggar.

When Decius was come again he commanded
that they should be fetched. And then Malchus,
which was their servant and ministered to them
meat and drink, returned in great dread to his
fellows and told and shewed to them the furour
and woodness of the Emperor. And then were
they sore afeard. And Malchus set tofore them
the loaves of bread that he had bought, so that
they were comforted of the meat and were more
strong for to suffer torments. And when they
had taken their refection and sat in weeping and
wailings, suddenly, as God would, they slept.
And when it came on the morrow they were
sought and could not be found: wherefore Decius
was sorrowful because he had lost such young
men. And then they were accused that they
were hid in the Mount of Caelion and had given
their goods to poor men, and yet abode in their
purpose. And then commanded Decius that their
kindred should come to him, and menaced them
to the death if they said not of them all that they
knew. And they accused them and complained
that they had despended all their riches. Then
Decius thought what he would do with them, and,
as Our Lord would, he enclosed the mouth of the
cave wherein they were with stones to the end

that they should die therein for hunger and default of meat. Then the ministers and two Christian men, Theodore and Ruffinus, wrote their martyrdom and laid it subtilly among the stones.

And when Decius was dead and all that generation, three clxxii years after, and the xxxth year of Theodosius the Emperor, when the heresy was of them that denied the resurrection of dead bodies and began to grow, Theodosius, then the most Christian emperor, being sorrowful that the faith of Our Lord was feloniously demeaned, for anger and heaviness he clad him in hair and wept every day in a secret place, and led a full holy life. Which God merciful and piteous seeing, would comfort them that were sorrowful and weeping, and give to them esperance and hope of the resurrection of dead men, and opened the precious treasure of His pity and raised the foresaid martyrs in this manner following.

He put in the will of a burgess of Ephesus that he would make in that mountain which was desert and asper a stable for his pastors and herdmen. And it happed that of adventure the masons that made the said stable opened this cave. And then these holy saints that were within awoke and were raised and inter-saluted each other, and had supposed verily that they had slept but one night only, and remembered of the heaviness that they had the day before. And then Malchus which ministered to them said what Decius had ordained of them. For he said, "We have been sought like as I said to you yes-

terday for to do sacrifice to the idols that is that
the Emperor desireth of us. And then Maximian answered, "God our Lord knoweth that
we shall never do sacrifice," and comforted his
fellows. He commanded to Malchus to go and
buy bread in the city, and bade him bring more
than he did yesterday, and also to enquire and
demand what the Emperor had commanded to
do.

And then Malchus took v. shillings and issued
out of the cave. And when he saw the masons
and the stones tofore the cave, he began to bless
him and was much amarvelled; but he thought
little of the stones for he thought on other things.
Then came he all doubtous to the gates of the
city and was all marvelled for he saw the sign of
the cross about the gate. And then without tarrying he went to that other gate of the city and
found there also the sign of the cross thereon.
And then he had great marvel for upon every
gate he saw set up the sign of the cross and
therewith the city was garnished. And then he
blessed him and returned to the first gate and
weened he had dreamed. And after, he advised
and comforted himself and covered his visage and
entered into the city. And when he came to
the sellers of bread and heard the men speak of
God, yet then was he more abashed, and said,
"What is this, that no man yesterday durst name
Jesus Christ and now every man confesseth him
to be Christian? I trow this is not the city of
Ephesus for it is all otherwise builded. It is

some other city I wot not what." And when he demanded and heard verily that it was Ephesus, he supposed that he had erred and thought verily to go again to his fellows. And then he went to them that sold bread and when he shewed his money the sellers marvelled and said that one to that other that this young man had found some old treasure. And when Malchus saw them talk together, he doubted not that they would lead him to the Emperor and was sore afeard and prayed them to let him go and keep both money and bread. But they held him and said to him, " Of whence art thou ? For thou hast founden treasure of the old emperors. Shew it to us and we shall be fellows with thee and keep it secret." And Malchus was so afeard that he wist not what to say to them for dread. And when they saw that he spake not, they put a cord about his neck and drew him through the city into the middle. And tidings were had all about in the city that a young man had found ancient treasure, in such wise that all they of the city assembled about him. And he confessed there that he had founden no treasure. And he beheld them all, but he could not know no man there of his kin-dred nor lineage, which he had verily supposed that they had lived, but he found none. Where-fore he stood as he had been from himself, in the middle of the city.

And when Saint Martin the bishop and Anti-pater the consul, which were new come into this city, heard of this thing they sent for him that they should bring him wisely to them and his money with him. And when he was brought to the church, he weened well he should have been led to the Emperor Decius. And then the bishop and the consul marvelled of the money, and they demanded him where he had found this treasure unknown. And he answered that he had no thing found, but it was come to him of his kindred and patrimony. And they demanded of him of what city he was. "I wot well that I am of this city, if this be the city of Ephesus." And the judge said to him, "Let thy kindred come and witness for thee." And he named them but none knew them. And they said that he feigned for to escape from them in some manner. And then said the judge, "How may we believe thee that this money is come to thee of thy friends, when it appeareth in the scripture that it is more than ccclxxii. years since it was made and forged, and it is of the first days of Decius the emperor, and it resembleth no thing to our money. And how may it come from thy lineage so long since, and thou art young? Thou wouldest deceive the wise and ancient men of this city of Ephesus. And therefore I command that thou be demeaned after the law till that thou hast confessed where thou hast found this money." Then Malchus kneeled down tofore them and said: "For God's sake, lords, say ye to me that I shall demand you and I shall tell to you all that I have in my heart Decius the emperor that was in this city where is he?" And the bishop said to him, "Son, there is no such at this day in the world that is named Decius : he was emperor many years since." And Malchus said, "Sir, hereof I am greatly abashed and no man believeth me. For I wot well that we fled for fear of Decius the emperor. And I saw him that yesterday he entered into this city if this be the city of Ephesus." Then the bishop thought in himself and said to the judge that this is a vision that Our Lord will have shewed by this young man. Then said the young man : "Follow ye me and I shall shew to you my fellows which be in the mount of Caelion, and believe ye them. This know I well that we fled from the face of the Emperor Decius." And then they went with him and a great multitude of people of the city with them. And Malchus entered first in to the cave of his fellows and the bishop next after him. And there found they among the stones the letters sealed with two seals of silver. And then the bishop called them that were come thither and read them tofore them all, so that they that heard it were all abashed and amarvelled. And they saw the saints sitting in the cave and their visages like unto roses flowering. And they kneeling down glorified God.

And anon the bishop and the judge sent to Theodosius the Emperor, praying him that he would come anon for to see the marvels of Our Lord that He had late shewed. And anon he arose up from the ground and took off the sack in which he wept and glorified Our Lord and came from Constantinople to Ephesus. And all they

came against him and ascended into the mountain
with him together unto the saints in to the cave.
And as soon as the blessed saints of Our Lord saw
the Emperor come their visages shone like to the
sun. And the Emperor entered then and glorified Our Lord and embraced them, weeping upon
each of them, and said, "I see you now like as I
should see Our Lord raising Lazarus." And then
Maximian said to him, "Believe us : for forsooth
Our Lord hath raised us tofore the day of the
great resurrection. And to the end that thou
believe firmly the resurrection of the dead people,
verily we be raised as ye here see, and live."
And when they had said all this, they inclined
their heads to the earth and rendered their spirits
at the commandment of Our Lord Jesus Christ
and so died. Then the Emperor arose and fell
on them weeping strongly and embraced them
and kissed them debonairly. And then he commanded to make precious sepulchres of gold and
silver and to bury their bodies therein. And in
the same night they appeared to the Emperor
and said to him that he should suffer them to lie
on the earth like as they had lain tofore, till that
time that Our Lord had raised them, unto the
time that they should rise again. Then commanded the Emperor that the place should be
adorned nobly and richly with precious stones.
It is doubt of that which is said that they slept
ccclxii. years. For they were raised the year of
Our Lord IIIICLXXXIII. And Decius reigned
but one year and three months and that was in

the year of our Lord CC and LXX., and so they slept but iic. and viii. years.

On an Easter day, when Saint Edward, the King of England and Confessor, had received Our Lord, and was set at his dinner, in the middle of it, when all was silence, he fell in to a smiling, and after in to a sadness, wherefore all that were there marvelled greatly, but none durst ask of him what he meant. But after dinner Duke Harold followed him into his chamber with a bishop and an abbot that were of his privy council, and demanded of him the cause of that thing. Then the king said, " When I remembered at my dinner the great benefits of worship and the dignity of meats, of drinks, of servants, of array, and of all riches and royalty that I stood in at that time, and I referred all that worship to Almighty God, as my custom is, then Our Lord opened mine eyes and I saw the seven sleepers lying in a cave in the Mount Caelion beside the city of Ephesus, in the same form and manner as though I had been by them. And I smiled when I saw them turn from the right side to the left side, but when I understood what it signified by the said turning I had no cause to laugh but rather to mourn. The turning signifieth that the prophecy be fulfilled which saith, 'Surget gens contra gentem,' that is to say, 'People shall arise against people and a kingdom against another.' They have lain many years upon their right side, and they shall lie yet upon their left side lxx. years, in which time shall be great battles, great pestilence, and great murrain, great earthquakes, great hunger and great dearth throughout all the world." Of which saying of the king they greatly marvelled. And anon they sent to the Emperor to know if there were any such city or hill in his land in which such seven men should sleep. Then the Emperor marvelling, sent to the same hill, and there found the cave and the seven martyrs sleeping as they had been dead, lying on the left side every one. And then the Emperor was greatly abashed at that sight, and commended greatly the holiness of Saint Edward, the King of England, which had the spirit of prophecy. For after his death began great insurrections through all the world. For the paynims destroyed a great part of Syria and threw down both monasteries and churches, and what by pestilence and stroke of sword, streets, fields and towns, lay full of dead men. The Prince of Greece was slain, the Emperor of Rome was slain, the King of England and the King of France were slain, and all the other realms of the world were greatly troubled with divers diseases.

THE holy cross was founden two hundred years after the resurrection of Our Lord. It is read in the gospel of Nicodemus, that when Adam waxed sick, Seth his son went to the gate of Paradise terrestrial for to get the oil of mercy for to anoint withal his father's body. Then appeared to him Saint Michael the angel and said to him, "Travail not in vain for this oil, for thou mayest not have it till five thousand and five hundred years been passed." (Howbeit that from Adam unto the passion of Our Lord were but five MC. and XXXIII. years.) In another place it is read that the angel brought him a branch, and commanded him to plant it in the Mount of Lebanon. Yet find we in another place that he gave to him of the tree that Adam ate of, and said to him that when that bare fruit, he should be guarished and all whole. When Seth came again he found his father dead and planted this tree upon his grave : and it endured there unto the time of Solomon. And because Solomon saw that it was fair he did do hew it down and set it in his house. And when the Queen of Sheba came to visit Solomon,

she worshipped this tree by cause she said the
Saviour of all the world should be hanged thereon, by whom the realm of the Jews shall be de-
faced and cease.   Solomon for this cause made it
to be taken up and buried deep in the ground.
Now it happed after that they of Jerusalem did
do make a great pit for a pool, whereas the ministers of the temple should wash their beasts that
they should sacrifice : and there found they this
tree.   And this piscine had such virtue that the
angels descended and moved the water and the
first sick man that descended into the water was
made whole of what somever sickness he was
sick of.   And when the time approached of the
Passion of Our Lord, this tree arose out of the
water and floated above the water.   And of this
piece of timber made the Jews the cross of Our
Lord.   Then, after this history, the cross by
which we be saved came of the tree by which
we were damned.   And the water of that piscine
had not his virtue only of the angel but of the
tree.   With this tree whereof the cross was made,
there was a tree that went overthwart on which
the arms of Our Lord were nailed : and another
piece above which was the table wherein the title
was written : and another piece wherein the
socket or mortice was made that the body of the
cross stood in.   So that there were four manner
of trees, that is, of palm, of cypress, of cedar, and
of olive.   So each of these four pieces was of
one of these trees.   This blessed cross was put
in the earth and hid, by the space of an c. year

and more. But the mother of the Emperor which was named Helena found it.

The virtue of the cross is declared to us by many miracles. For it happed on a time that one enchanter had deceived a notary and brought him into a place where he had assembled a great company of devils, and promised to him that he would make him to have much riches. And when he came there he saw one person black sitting on a great chair, and all about him all full of horrible people and black which had spears and swords. Then demanded this great devil of the enchanter who was that clerk. The enchanter said to him, "Sir, he is ours." Then said the devil to him, "If thou wilt worship me and be my servant and reny Jesus Christ thou shalt sit on my right side." The clerk anon blessed him with the sign of the cross, and said that he was the servant of Jesus Christ his Saviour. And anon as he had made the cross that great multitude of devils vanished away.

At Constantinople a Jew entered in to the Church of Saint Sophia and considered that he was there alone, and saw an image of Jesus Christ and took his sword and smote the image in the throat and anon the blood gushed out and sprang in the face and on the head of the Jew. And he then was afeared and took the image and cast it into a pit and anon fled away. And it happed that a Christian man met him and saw him all bloody and said to him, "From whence comest thou? Thou hast slain some man." And he said, "I have not." The Christian man said, "Verily thou hast commised some homicide for thou art all besprongen with the blood." And the Jew said, "Verily the God of Christian men is great, and the faith of Him is firm and approved in all things. I have smitten no man but I have smitten the image of Jesus Christ and anon issued blood of his throat." And then the Jew brought the Christian man to the pit and there they drew out that holy image. And yet is seen on this day the wound in the throat of the image; and the Jew anon became a good Christian man and was baptized.

HE holy Saint Clement rehearseth in the sixth book of *Historia Ecclesiastica* that on a time Saint John the Evangelist converted to the faith a goodly young man, well favoured and strong, and commended him unto the keeping, rule, and governance of a bishop. And within a little while after this young man forsook the bishop and fell into evil company among thieves, and became and was made master and prince of them. Anon after the apostle came to the bishop and demanded for this young man; and the bishop was sore abashed. When Saint John saw his countenance he demanded more busily after him and where he had left him. "For I ask him of thee, whom I delivered to thee, and gave thee so great charge with him." Then said the bishop to him, "Father, truly he is dead in his soul, and is in yonder mountain with thieves, and is their master and prince." And when he heard this, for sorrow he rent his clothes and said to the bishop, "Thou art a feeble keeper, for to suffer thy brother to lose his soul." Anon he made a horse to be made ready for him and rode fast to the mountain. And when the young man espied and knew him he so was sore ashamed that he fled from him. Then the Apostle forgat his age and pricked after and cried after him that fled, "My most sweet son, why fleest thou 'from thy father, feeble and old. Be thou not afeard, son, for I shall yield accounts for thee to Jesus Christ. And truly I shall gladly die for thee, like as Jesus Christ died for us. Turn again, my son, turn again. Jesus Christ hath sent me to thee." And when he heard him thus speak, he abode with an heavy cheer and wept, repenting him bitterly, and fell down to the feet of the Apostle and for penance kissed his hand. And the Apostle fasted and prayed to God for him and gat for him remission of his sins and forgiveness. And he lived so virtuously after that Saint John ordained him to be a bishop.

It happed on a day that Crato the philosopher made a great assemble of people in the midst of the city, for to show them how they ought to despise the world. And he had ordained two young men, brethren, which were much rich, and had made them to sell their patrimony and therewith to buy precious stones. The which these two young men brake in the presence of the people for to shew how these precious and great riches of the world be soon destroyed. That same time, Saint John passed by and said to Crato the philosopher: "This manner for to despise the world that thou shewest is vain and foolish demonstrance. For it seeketh to have the praising of the world, and God reproveth it. My good

Master, Jesus Christ, said to a man that demanded
of Him how he might come into everlasting life,
that he should go and sell all his good, and give
that he received of it to the poor people, and he
should find treasure in heaven." Crato said then
to him: "The price and value of these precious
stones is destroyed in the presence of all men here.
But if thy master be very God, and He will that
the goods of the world be given to poor men, take
then the pieces of these precious stones and make
them whole stones as they were tofore. Because
if I have shewed this vain-glory, make thou them
to the honour of thy Master." Anon Saint John
took the pieces of the precious stones.. And after
that he had made his prayer unto God, he shewed
to them the stones as whole as ever they were or
had been. When Crato the philosopher saw this,
anon he with his two men and his disciples fell
down to the feet of Saint John and received the
faith and baptism of Jesus Christ, and sold the
precious stones and gave the money thereof for
the love of God and began to preach the faith of
Our Lord and Saviour, Jesus Christ.

Cassiodorus saith that a man had given to Saint
John a partridge living, and he held it in his hand,
stroking and playing with it other while for his
recreation. And on a time, a young man passed
by with his fellowship and saw him play with his
bird. Which said to his fellows, laughing: "See
how the yonder old man playeth with a bird like
a child." Which Saint John knew anon by the

Holy Ghost what he had said, and called the young man to him and demanded him what he held in his hand, and he said a bow. "What dost thou withal?" said Saint John. And the young man said, "We shoot birds and beasts therewith." To whom the Apostle demanded how and in what manner. Then the young man bent his bow and held it in his hand bent; and when the Apostle said no more to him, he unbent his bow again. Then said the Apostle to him, "Why hast thou unbent thy bow?" And he said, "Because if it should be long bent, it should be the weaker for to shoot with it." Then said the Apostle, "So, son, it fareth by mankind. By frailty in contemplation, if it should alway be bent, it should be too weak and therefore otherwhile it is expedient to have recreation. The eagle is the bird that flieth highest and most clearly beholdeth the sun, and yet by necessity of nature him behoveth to descend low. Right so, when mankind withdraweth him a little from contemplation, he after putteth himself higher by a renewed strength, and he burneth then more fervently in heavenly things.

There was a king, an holy confessor and virgin, named Saint Edward, which had a special devotion unto Saint John the Evangelist. And it happed that this holy king was at the hallowing of a church dedicate in the honour of God and of this holy Apostle. And it was so that Saint John in likeness of a pilgrim came to this king and demanded him alms in the name of Saint John.

ST. JOHN THE EVANGELIST.

And the king not having his almoner by him nor
his chamberlain of whom he might have somewhat to give him took his ring which he bare on
his finger and gave it to the pilgrim. After this
many days, it happened two pilgrims of England
for to be in the Holy Land. And Saint John
appeared to them and bade them to bear this ring
to their king and to greet him well in his name ;
and to tell him that he gave it to Saint John in
likeness of a pilgrim and that he should make him
ready to depart out of this world ; for he should
not long abide here, but come in to everlasting
bliss. And so vanished from them. And anon
as he was gone they had great lust to sleep and
laid them down and slept. And this was in the
Holy Land. And when they awoke they looked
about them and knew not where they were. And
they saw flocks of sheep, and shepherds keeping
them, to whom they went to know the way and
to demand where that they were. And when
they asked them, they spake English and said that
they were in England in Kent on Barham Down.
And then they thanked God and Saint John for
their good speed, and came to this holy king
Saint Edward on Christmas Day and delivered to
him the ring and did their errand. Whereof the
king was abashed and thanked God and the holy
saint that he had warning for to depart. And on
the vigil of the Epiphany next after he died and
departed holily out of this world and is buried in
the Abbey of Westminster by London whereas is
yet unto this day that same ring.

AINT MARTHA, hostess of Our Lord Jesus Christ, was born of a royal kindred. Her father was named Syrus and her mother Eucharia. The father of her was duke of Syria and the maritime parts, and Martha with her sister possessed by the heritage of their mother three places, that was the Castle Magdala and, Bethany and a part of Jerusalem. It is no where read that Martha had ever any husband nor fellowship of man. But she as a noble hostess ministered and served Our Lord, and would also that her sister should serve Him and help her, for she thought that all the world was not sufficient to serve such a guest.

After the ascension of Our Lord, when the disciples were departed, she with her brother Lazarus and her sister Mary, also Saint Maximin, which baptized them, and to whom they were committed of the Holy Ghost, and many other, were put in to a ship without sail, oars or other governal, of the paynims. By the conduct of Our Lord they came to Marseilles, and after came to the territory of Aix, and there converted the people to the faith. Martha was right fair of speech and courteous and gracious to the sight of the people.

ST. MARTHA.

There was that time upon the river of Rhone in a certain wood between Arles and Avignon a great dragon, half beast and half fish, greater than an ox, longer than a horse, having teeth sharp as a sword, and horned on either side, head like a lion, tail like a serpent. And he defended him with two wings on either side, and could not be beaten with casting of stones nor with other armour, and was as strong as twelve lions or bears. Which dragon lay hiding and lurking in the river, and perished them that passed by, and drowned ships. He came thither by sea from Galatia in Asia, and was engendered of leviathan, which is a serpent of the water and is much wood, and of a beast called Bonacho, that is engendered in Galatia. And when he is pursued, he casteth out of his belly behind his ordure, for the space of an acre land, on them that follow him, and it is bright as glass, and what it toucheth it burneth as fire.

To whom Martha at the prayer of the people came in to the wood, and found him eating a man. And she cast on him holy water and shewed to him the cross. Anon he was overcome and, standing still as a sheep, she bound him with her own girdle, and then he was slain with spears and glaives of the people. The dragon was called of them that dwelt in the country Tarasconus, wherefore in remembrance of him that place is called Tarascon, which before was called Nerluc and the Black Lake, by cause there be woods shadowous and black.

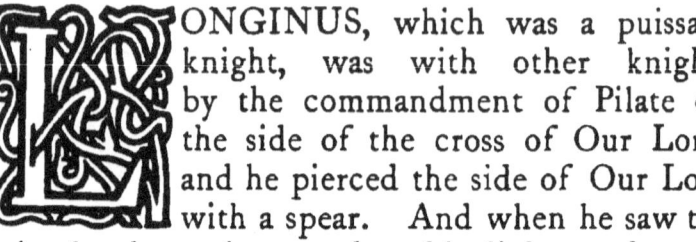ONGINUS, which was a puissant knight, was with other knights by the commandment of Pilate on the side of the cross of Our Lord, and he pierced the side of Our Lord with a spear. And when he saw the miracles how the sun lost his light, and great earth quaking of the earth was, when Our Lord suffered death and passion in the tree of the cross, then believed he in Jesus Christ. Some say that when he smote Our Lord with the spear in the side, the precious blood descended by the shaft of the spear upon his hands, and of adventure with his hands he touched his eyes, and anon he that had been tofore blind saw anon clearly. Wherefore he refused all chivalry and abode with the apostles, of whom he was taught and christened, and after he abandoned to lead an holy life in doing alms and in keeping the life of a monk about xxxviii. years in Caesarea and Cappadocia, and by his words and his example many men converted he to the faith of Christ.

T is read in a history, though it be named apocrypha, that there was a man in Jerusalem named Reuben and by another name Simeon. of the kindred of David, or, after Saint Jerome, of the tribe of Issachar, which had a wife named Ciborea. And on the night that Judas was conceived his mother had a marvellous dream whereof she was sore afeard. For her seemed that she had conceived a child that should destroy their people. And by cause thereof her husband blamed her much, and said to her, "Thou sayest a thing over evil, or the devils will to deceive thee." She said, "Certainly, if so be that I shall have a son, I trow it shall be so, as I have had a revelation and none illusion." When the child was born the father and mother were in great doubt and thought what was best to do, for they durst not slay the child for the horror that they should have therein, neither they wist not how they might nourish one that should destroy their lineage. Then they put him to a little basket well pitched, and set it in the sea, and abandoned him to drive whither it would. And anon the floods and waves of the sea brought and made him arrive in an island named Scarioth, and of this name was he called Judas Iscariot. Now it happed that the queen of this country went to play on the rivage of the sea and beheld this little vessel and a child therein which was fair. And then she sighed and said, "O Lord God, how should I be eased if I had such a child, then at least should not my realm be without heir." Then commanded she that the child should be taken up, and be nourished, and she feigned herself to be great with child, and after published that she had borne a fair son. When her husband heard say hereof, he had great joy and all the people of the country made great feast. The king and queen did do nourish and keep this child like the son of a king. Anon after it happened that the queen conceived a son. And when it was born and grown, Judas beat often that child, for he weened that he had been his brother. And oft he was chastised therefore, but alway he made him to weep so long, that the queen which knew well that Judas was not her son, at last she said the truth, and told how that Judas was found in the sea. And ere this yet was known, Judas slew the child that he had supposed to be his brother and was son to the king. And in eschewing the sentence of death he fled anon and came in to Jerusalem, and entered into the court of Pilate which then was provost. And he so pleased him that he was great with him, and had in great charity and nothing was done without him.

Now it happed on a day that Pilate went for to

disport him by a garden belonging to the father
of Judas, and was so desirous to eat of the fruit of
the apples that he might not forbear them. And
the father of Judas knew not his son Judas, for he
had supposed that he had been drowned in the
sea long to fore, nor the son the father. When
Pilate had told to Judas of his desire, he sprang in
to the garden of his father, and gathered of the
fruit for to bear to his master. But the father of
Judas defended him, and there began between
them much strife and debate, first by words and
after with fighting. So much, that Judas smote
his father with a stone on the head that he slew
him, and after brought the apples unto Pilate, and
told to him how that he had slain him that ought
the garden. Then sent Pilate to seize all the
goods that the father of Judas had and after gave
his wife to Judas in marriage, and thus Judas
wedded his own mother.

Now it happed on a day that the lady wept and
sighed much strongly and said, "Alas! how un-
happy that I am, I have lost my son and my husband. My son was laid on the sea and I suppose
that he be drowned, and my husband is dead suddenly. And yet it is more grievous to me that
Pilate hath re-married me against my will." Then
demanded Judas of this child. And she told him
how he was set on the sea. And Judas told to
her how he had been founden on the sea; in such
wise that she wist that she was his mother and
that he had slain his father and wedded his mother.
Wherefore then he went to Jesus Christ, which

did so many miracles, and prayed Him of mercy and forgiveness of his sins. Thus far is it read in the history which is not authentic.

PILATE.

Of the pain of Pilate and his birth thou shalt find in one apocryphum, where as it is said in this manner:

There was a king called Tyrus which knew carnally a maid called Pila, which was daughter of a miller named Atus. And of this daughter he engendered a son. She took her name and the name of her father which was called Atus, and composed thus of their names one name to her son and named him Pilatus. And when he was three years old she sent him to the king. And the king had a son of the queen which seemed to be of the age of Pilate. And these two sons when they were of age of discretion, oft they fought together and with the sling they played oft. And the king's son also which was legitimate, was more noble, and in all feats he knew more, and more was set by by cause of his birth. And Pilate seeing this was moved of envy and wrath and privily slew his brother. The which thing the king heard say, and was much angry and demanded of his council what he might do and make of this trespass and homicide. The which all with one voice said that he was worthy to suffer death. And the king would not double the pain and punition to himself, but by cause he ought to the Romans yearly a tribute, he sent him

in hostage to the Romans as well for to be quit
of the death of his son, as that he should not be
constrained to put him to death, and for to be
quit of the tribute that he ought to Rome. And
this time was at Rome one of the sons of the
King of France which also was sent for tribute.
And when Pilate saw him he anon accompanied
with him, and when he saw that he was praised
tofore him for the wit and for the manners that
were in him, Pilate slew him also. And when
the Romans demanded what should be done in
this matter, they answered that he which had
slain his brother, and estrangled him that was in
hostage, if he might live should be yet much
profitable to the common weal, and should daunt
the necks of them that were cruel and wood.
And then said the Romans that since he was
worthy to die he should be sent in to an isle of
the sea named Pontus to them that will suffer no
judge over them, to the end that his wickedness
may overcome and judge them or else that he
suffer of them like as he hath deserved.

Then was Pilate sent to this cruel people and
wild which tofore had slain their judge. And it
was told to him to what people he was sent and
that he should consider how his life was hanging
and in great jeopardy. He went considering his
life and, thinking to keep it, did so much what
by menaces and promises and torment, as by
gifts, that he subdued them all and put them in
subjection. And by cause he had victory of this
cruel people, he was named of this Isle of Pontus,

Pontius Pilate. And when Herod heard his iniquities and his frauds he had great joy thereof. And by cause he was wicked himself he would have the wicked with him and sent for him by messengers and by promise of gifts that he came to him and gave him the power upon the realm of Judæa and Jerusalem. And when he had assembled and gathered together much money, he went to Rome without knowing of Herod, and offered right great sums of money for to get to himself that which Herod so held. And so he gat it. And for this cause Herod and Pilate were enemies unto the time of the Passion of Jesus Christ, whom Pilate sent to prison.

And when Pilate had delivered Jesus Christ to the Jews for to be crucified he doubted the Emperor that he should be reproved of that he 'had judged an innocent, and sent a friend of his for to excuse him. And in this while Tiberius the Emperor fell into a grievous malady. And it was told to him that there was one in Jerusalem that cured all manner maladies, and he knew not that Pilate and the Jews had slain Him. He said to Volusian, which was secret with him, "Go in to the parts over sea, and say to Pilate that he send to me the leech or master in medicine for to heal me of my malady." And when he wss come to Pilate and had said his message, Pilate was much abashed and demanded xiii days of dilation within which time Volusian found on old woman named Veronica which had been familiar and devout with Jesus Christ. He demanded of her where he might find Him that he sought. She then cried and said, "Alas, Lord God, my Lord, my God was He that ye ask for, whom Pilate damned to death, and whom the Jews delivered to Pilate for envy and commanded that He should be crucified." Then he complained him sorrowfully and said, "I am sorry by cause he may not accomplish that which my lord the Emperor hath charged me." To whom Veronica said, "My Lord and my Master when He went preaching, I absented me oft from Him, so I did do paint His visage, for to have alway with me His presence, by cause that the figure of His image hould give me some solace. And then as I bare a linen kerchief in my bosom, Our Lord met me and demanded whither I went and when I had told him whither I went and the cause, He demanded the kerchief, and anon He imprinted His face and figured it therein. And if thy lord had beholden the figure of Jesus Christ devoutly he should be anon guarished and healed. And Volusian asked, "Is there neither gold nor silver that this figure may be bought with?" She answered, "Nay, but strong of courage, devout and of great affection, I shall go with thee and shall bear it to the Emperor for to see it, and after I shall return hither again." Then went Volusian with Veronica to Rome, and said to the Emperor, "Jesus of Nazareth, whom thou hast long desired, Pilate and the Jews by envy and with wrong have put to death and have hanged him on the cross. And a

matron, a widow, is come with me which bringeth
the image of Jesus, the which if thou with good
heart and devoutly wilt behold and have therein
contemplation, thou shalt anon be whole." And
when the Emperor had heard this, he did anon
make ready the way with clothes of silk, and
made the image of Jesus to be brought to fore
him. And anon as he had seen it and worshipped
it, he was all guarished and whole.

Then, when the Emperor heard that Pilate was
come to Rome, he was much wroth and inflamed
against him, and bad that he should be brought
tofore him. Pilate wore alway the garment of
Our Lord, which was without seam, wherewith
he was clad when he came tofore the Emperor.
And as soon as the Emperor saw him all his wrath
was gone and the ire out of his heart, he could
not say an evil word to him. And in his absence
he was sore cruel towards him, and in his presence
he was alway sweet and debonair to him, and gave
him licence and he departed. And anon as he
departed he was as angry and as sore moved as he
was tofore, and more by cause he had not shewed
to him his fury. Then he made him to be called
again and sware he should be dead. And anon as
he saw him his cruelty was all gone, whereof was
great marvel. Now was there one by the inspiration of God, or at the persuasion of some Christian
man, that caused the Emperor to despoil him of
that coat. And anon as he had put it off, the
Emperor had in his heart as great ire and fury as
he had to fore, wherefore the Emperor marvelled

at this coat and it was told to him that it was the
coat of Jesus. Then the Emperor made Pilate to
be set in prison till he had counselled what he
should do with him, and sentence was given that
he should die a villanous death. And when Pilate
heard the sentence he took a knife and slew himself. And when the Emperor heard how he was
dead, he said, "Certainly he is dead of a right
villanous death and foul, for his own proper hand
hath not spared him." Then his body was taken
and bounden to a mill-stone and was cast in the
river of Tiber for to be sunken to the bottom.
And the ill spirits in the air began to move great
tempests and marvellous waves in the water, and
horrible thunder and lightning, whereof the people
was sore afraid and in great doubt. And therefore
the Romans drew out the body and in derision
sent it to Vienne and cast it into the river named
Rhone. Vienne is as much to say as hell, which
is said Gehenna, for then it was accused place,
and so there is his body in the place of maledic-
tion. And the evil spirits been as well there as
in other places, and made such tempests as they
did before, in so much that they of that place
might not suffer it. And therefore they took the
vessel wherein the body was and sent it for to
bury it in the territory of the city of Losane.*
And it was taken thence and thrown into a deep
pit all environed with mountains. In which
place, after the relation of some, be seen illusions,
and machinations of fiends be seen to grow and

* Lausanne or Lucerne.

boil.   And hitherto is the history called apocryphum read: They that have read this let them say
and believe as it shall please them.

JULIAN there was that was no saint but a cursed man, and was called Julianus Apostata. This Julian was first a monk and shewing outward signs of great religion and of great holiness, after that that Master John Beleth reciteth. There was a woman that had three pots full of gold, and by cause the gold should not be seen she had put in the mouth of the pots above ashes, and delivered them to this Julian tofore other monks for to keep, whom she reputed an holy man : but she said not to him that they were full of gold. When he had these pots he looked what was therein and he found that it was gold, and took it out all, and filled them full of ashes, and fled withal to Rome. And he did so much that he was of the councillors and governors of Rome. But the woman, when she would have again her pots, she could not prove that she had delivered to him in keeping gold, for she made no mention thereof tofore the monks, and therefore he retained it, and procured withal the office of a consul of the governance of Rome. And after that he procured so much that he was instituted emperor.

Whiles he was young he was taught in the art of enchantment and of the invocation of fiends.

And gladly he studied it and it pleased him much
and he had with him divers masters of the science.
Now it happed on a day that, as his master was
out, he began alone to read the invocations, and a
great multitude of fiends came about him and
made him afeard. And he made the sign of the
cross and anon they vanished away. And when
his master was returned, he told him what was
happened to him. But his master said to him that
alway he had hated and feared that sign. Then
when he was emperor he remembered thereof and,
because he would use the craft of the devil over
all, where he found the signs of the cross he destroyed them, and persecuted the Christian men
because that he knew well that otherwise the
fiends would not do for him.

And, as it is read in the history of Saint Basil, he
came into Caesarea of Cappadocia and Saint Basil
came against him and presented three loaves to
him. And Julian had great indignation of this
gift and for the bread he sent to Saint Basil hay
saying, "Thou hast sent to me meat for dumb
beasts, therefore take this that I send to thee."
Saint Basil said, "We have sent to thee such as
we eat and thou sendest to us of that thou
nourishest thy beasts with." Of which answer
Julian was wroth and said, "When I shall have
done in Persia, I shall destroy this city in such
wise that it shall be better ordained for to ear and
sow than for people to dwell in." And the
night ensuing Saint Basil saw in a vision in the
church of Our Lady a great multitude of angels,

and, in the middle of them, a woman being on a throne which said to them, "Call to me Mercury whom Julian the apostata hath slain, which blasphemeth me and my son." Mercury was a knight that for the faith of God had been slain of Julian and was buried in the same church. Then anon Mercury with all his arms that were kept, was present; and at the commandment of the lady he went to battle. Saint Basil awoke all afraid and went to the tomb where the knight was buried in and opened the sepulchre but he found neither body nor arms. Then he demanded of the keeper who had taken away the body. And he sware that in the evening tofore it was there. Saint Basil after on the morrow returned and found the body and the armour and the spear all bloody. And anon came one from the battle which said that Julian the apostata and emperor was in the battle and thither came a knight unknown all armed, with his spear. Which hardily smote his horse with his spurs and came to Julian the emperor, and brandished his sword and smote him through the body, and suddenly he departed, and never after was seen. And when Julian should die, he took his hand full of blood and cast it into the air, saying, "Thou hast vanquished, man of Galilee, thou hast overcome." And in crying thus miserably, he expired and died in great pain and was left without sepulchre of all his men. And he was flayed of the Persians and of his skin was made to the king of Persia an under-covering and thus he died cursedly.

AINT MACARIUS was in a desert and entered into a pit or sepulture, where as had been buried many bodies of paynims, for to sleep. And he drew out one of these bodies and laid it under his head instead of a pillow. Then came thither devils for to make him aghast and afeared, and said one to another, "Come with me to bathe thee." And the body that lay under his head said, "I may not come for I have a pilgrim upon me lying that I may not move." For all this Saint Macarius was not afeard, but he beat the body with his fist and said, "Arise and go if thou canst." When the devils saw that they might not make him afeard, they cried with a great voice, "Macarius thou hast vanquished and overcome us."

On a time as Macarius was nigh his house, the the devil came with a great scythe on his neck and would have smitten therewith Saint Macarius. And the devil said to him, "Thou doest to me great violence and force for I may not prevail against thee. Lo, what thou doest I do. Thou fastest and I eat not. Thou wakest and I never sleep. But there is one thing in which thou overcomest me." And Macarius said, "What is that?" To whom the devil said, "That is humility and thy meekness by which I may not prevail against thee." It happened on a time that a great temptation came upon Saint Macarius, and much tempted him. And anon he filled a sack full of stones and laid it on his neck and bare it many journeys together through the desert. Then another hermit met him and demanded him why he bare so great a burden, and he answered, " I travail my body because it suffereth me not in peace, and thus I vex him that vexed me." Another time Saint Macarius met the devil and demanded him whence he came. And the devil answered, " I come from visiting thy brethren." Then said Saint Macarius, " How do they ? " The devil answered, " Evil." And he asked wherefore, and the devil said, " For they be all holy, and the worst of it, there was one that was mine, and I have lost him, for he is now made holier than the others." When Saint Macarius heard this, he gave lovings and thankings to God.

It happed on a time Saint Macarius found in his way the head of a dead man, and he demanded of it whose head it was. And the head answered, " Of a paynim." And Macarius said to him, " Where is thy soul ? " He answered, " In hell." And he demanded if it were deep in hell. And he said, " Deeper than is from heaven to earth." And after he demanded if there were any beneath him. And he said the Jews be lower than he was. He asked if there were any lower or beneath the Jews. To whom he said that the false Christian men be yet lower and deeper in hell than the Jews; for as much as they have despised and villanied the blood of Jesus Christ of which they were redeemed, so much the more be they tormented.

On a time Saint Macarius went in a desert and at the end of every mile he set a reed in the earth for to have knowledge thereby to turn again; and went forth ix. days journey and after he slept. And the devil took all these reeds and bound them and laid them at his head. Wherefore he had great labour for to come again in to his house.

It happed on a time that Saint Macarius killed a fly that bit him. And when he saw the blood of this fly he repented him, and so, repentant of that, would revenge it, and anon unclothed him and went naked in the desert vi. months, and suffered himself to be bitten of the flies.

ELIX was surnamed "in pincis" and it is said of the place where he resteth or of the pointels of "greffes" (graphs): a "greffe" is properly called a pointel to write in tables of wax, by which he suffered death. And some say that he was a schoolmaster and taught children and was to them much rigorous. After he was known of the paynims and because he confessed plainly that he was Christian and believed in Jesus Christ, he was delivered to be tormented into the hands of the children his scholars whom he had taught and learned, which scholars slew him with their pointels, pricks and greffes. And yet the church holdeth him for no martyr, but for a confessor. And the paynims said to him that he should do sacrifice to the idols; but he blew on them and anon they fell to the the earth.

It is read in a legend that, when Maximus bishop and Valerian fled the persecution of the pagans, the bishop was tormented with hunger and thirst so much that he fell down to the ground. Wherefore Felix was sent of an angel to him and he bare nothing with him for to give him. And he saw hy him a cluster of raisins hanging on a tree, which he laid on his shoulders hastily and bare it with him. And when the bishop was dead, Felix was elect and chosen bishop.

And as he preached on a time the persecutors sought him and he hid him in the clefts of a broken wall; and incontinent by the will of God came spiders and made their work and nets before him that they might not find him. And when the tyrants could not find him they went their way. And he went thence and came to the house of a widow, and took there his refection of her three months and yet he saw her never in the visage. And at the last, when the peace was made, he went unto his church and there died and rested in Our Lord and was buried by the city in a place that was called pincis.

HERE was sometime a tax-gatherer named Peter in a city, that was a much rich man : but he was not piteous but cruel to poor people : for he would hunt and chase alway poor people and beggars from his house with indignation and anger. Thus would no poor man come to him for alms. Then was there one poor man said to his fellows, "What will ye give me if I get of him an alms this day?" And they made a wager with him that he should not. Which done, he went to the tax-gatherer's house and stood at the gate and demanded alms. And when this rich man came and saw this poor man at his gate, he was much angry and would have cast somewhat at his head but could find no thing. At the last came one of his servants bearing a basket full of rye-bread, and in a great anger he took a rye loaf and threw it at his head as he that might not hear the cry of the poor man. And he took up the loaf and ran to his fellows and said truly that he had received that loaf of Peter's own hand. And then within two days after this rich man was sick and like to die. And as he lay he was ravished in spirit : in which he saw that he was set in judgment and black men brought forth his wicked deeds and laid

them in a balance on the one side. And on the
other side he saw some clothed in white mourning and sorrowful, but they had nothing to lay
against them in the other balance. And one of
them said, " Truly we have no thing but a rye
loaf which he gave to God against his will but
two days past." And then they put the loaf into
the balance. And him seemed the balances were
like even. Then they said to him, "Increase
and multiply this rye loaf or else thou must be
delivered to these black fiends." And when he
awoke he said, "Alas, if a rye loaf have so much
availed me that I gave in despite, how much
should it have availed me if I had given all my
goods to poor men with a good will."

As this rich man went on a day clothed with
his best clothes a poor shipman came to him all
naked and demanded of him some clothing for
the love of God to cover him withal; and he
anon despoiled himself and gave to him his rich
clothing that he wore. And anon the poor man
sold it. And when he knew that the poor man
had sold it, he was so sorry that he would eat no
meat, but he said, "Alas, I am not worthy that
the poor man think upon me." And the night
following, when he slept, he saw one brighter
than the sun having a cross on his head, wearing
the same cloth that he had given to the poor
man. And he said to him, "Why weepest thou,
toller?" And when he had told to him the
cause of his sorrow, he said to him, "Knowest
thou this cloth?" And he said, "Yea, sir."

And Our Lord said, "I have been clothed therewith since thou gavest it to me. And I thank thee of thy goodwill that thou haddest of my nakedness, for when I was a cold thou coveredst me." And when he awoke he blessed the poor people and said, "By the living God, if I live, I will be one His poor men."

And when he had given all his goods to poor men, he called one of his secret men whom he trusted well and said to him, "I have a secret counsel to tell thee. And if thou keep it not secret and do as I bid thee, I shall sell thee to the heathen ¡men." And he took him x pound in gold and bad him go in to the holy city and buy some mercer's ware. "And when thou hast so done, take me and sell me to some Christian man and take that money that thou shalt receive for me and give it to poor people." And the servant refused it. And he said, "Truly, if thou sell me not, I shall sell thee to the barbarians." And then he took this Peter the toller as he had commanded him, which was his master, and clad him in vile clothing and led him to the market and sold him to a money-changer for xxx. besants which he took and dealt it among the poor men.

This Peter then, thus sold, was bound and put into a kitchen for to do all foul works, in such wise that he was despised of every man of the servants. And some oft smote him and knocked him about the head and called him fool. Christ appeared oft to him and shewed him his clothing and the besants and comforted him.

And the Emperor and other people were sorry for the loss of Peter the Toller. And it happed that noble men of Constantinople came unto the place whereas Peter was for to visit holy places, whom the master of Peter had to dinner. And as they sat and ate at their dinner, Peter served and passed by them, and they beholding him said to each other in their ears, "How like is this young man to Peter the Toller." And as they well saw and advised him, they said, "Verily it is my lord Peter, I shall arise and hold him." And when Peter understood that, he fled away privily.

There was a porter which was both deaf and dumb and by signs he opened the gates. And Peter bad him by words to open the gate, and he anon heard him and receiving speech, answered him. And Peter went his way. And the porter returned into the house speaking and hearing, whereof all they marvelled. To whom he said, "He that was in the kitchen is gone out and fleeth away. But know ye for certain that he is the servant of God, for as he spake and bade me open the gate, there issued out of his mouth a flame of fire which touched my tongue and mine ears, and anon I received hearing and speaking." And anon they all went out, and ran after him, but they might not find him. Then all they of the house repented them and did penance, by cause they had so foul entreated him.

XXV.—THE INVENTION OF SAINT FIRMIN.

IN the time of the invention of Saint Firmin the martyr there was Saint Salvius Bishop of Amiens, and saw that tofore him in the time of Saint Honorius, Our Lord had done take up the bodies of Saint Fulgentius, Saint Victoricus, and Saint Gentius, and thought all an whole night upon the body of Saint Firmin the Martyr. And when it was day, this holy man Saint Salvius summoned the clergy and the people to fast and make prayers through the city of Amiens, to the end that Our Lord would shew them the place where the body of Saint Firman the martyr lay. And on the third day, Our Lord sent such a miracle that He sent a ray of the sun which pierced the wall of the monastery on the same side where the body lay. Then they began to dig and delve there. And when they came nigh the body there issued out so great a sweetness out of the pit that all they that were there weened they had been in Paradise: and it seemed that if all the spices of of the earth had been stamped together it should not have smelled so well nor so sweet. And this sweet odour spread through the city of Amiens and divers cities about, that is to wit Terwan, Cambrai and Noyon. And the people of these

cities moved them each from his place with candles
and offerings, without sayer or commander, but
only for the odour that so spread, and came unto
this glorious saint. And as the body was borne
in the city of Amiens, there were shewed such
miracles that never none were like found nor seen
tofore of any saint. For the elements moved them
by the miracles of this saint. The snow that was
that time great on the earth was turned into powder and dust by the heat that was then, and the
ice that hanged on the trees became flowers and
leaves, and the meadows about Amiens flowered
and became green. And the sun, which by his
nature should go low that day, ascended as high as
she is on Saint John's day at noon in the summer.
And as men bare the body of this saint, the trees
inclined and worshipped the body. And all
manner sick men, what malady they had, they received health in the invention of the blessed body
of Saint Firmin. And the burgesses that were in
their gowns and mantles had so great heat that
they called their servants and bondsmen, of whom
there were many that day in Amiens, and affran-
chised them, for to bear their clothes into the city
of Amiens. Our Lord did do shew such miracles
and so far sent the odour, that the lord of Beau-
gency, which was at a window and was sick of
lazarie, he smelled the odour and was anon guarished and whole. And he took his gold and came
and did homage unto the body of Saint Firmin in
the city of Amiens. Our Lord hath shewed many
miracles for this glorious saint, and much he ought

to be honoured in this world, and then pray we unto this blessed saint, Saint Firmin, that he pray for us to Our Lord that He will pardon us our sins, and bestow and grant to us the glory of heaven. Amen.

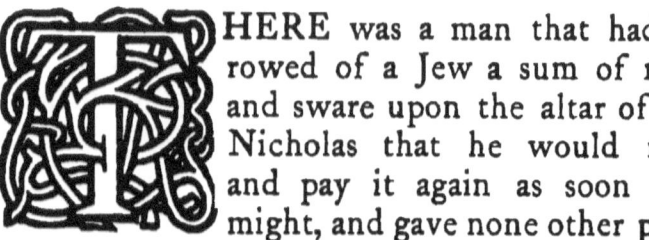

HERE was a man that had borrowed of a Jew a sum of money and sware upon the altar of Saint Nicholas that he would render and pay it again as soon as he might, and gave none other pledge. And this man held this money so long that the Jew demanded and asked his money. And he said that he had paid him. Then the Jew made him to come tofore the law in judgment, and the oath was given to the debtor. And he brought with him an hollow staff in which he had put the money in gold and he leant upon the staff. And when he should make his oath and swear, he delivered his staff to the Jew to keep and hold while he should swear. And then he sware that he had delivered to him more than he owed to him. And when he had made the oath he demanded his staff again of the Jew: and he, knowing nothing of his malice, delivered it to him. Then this deceiver went his way and anon after, him listed sore to sleep, and he laid him in the way. And a cart with four wheels came with great force, and slew him, and brake the staff with gold that it spread abroad. And when the Jew heard this, he came thither sore moved and saw the fraud. And many said that he should take to him the gold. And he refused it saying, "But if he that was dead were not raised again to life by the merits of Saint Nicholas, he would not receive it." Then he that was dead arose and the Jew was christened.

Another Jew saw the virtuous miracles of Saint Nicholas and did do make an image of the Saint and set it in his house. And he commanded him that he should keep well his house when he went out and that he should keep well all his goods, saying to him, "Nicholas, lo, here be all my goods. I charge thee to keep them. And if thou keep them not well, I shall avenge me on thee in beating and tormenting thee." And on a time when the Jew was out, thieves came and robbed all his goods and left unborne away only the image. And when the Jew came home he found him robbed of all his goods. He areasoned the image, saying these words, "Sir Nicholas, I had set you in my house for to keep my goods from thieves. Wherefore have you not kept them. Ye shall receive sorrow and torments and shall have pain for the thieves. I shall avenge my loss and refrain my woodness in beating thee." And then took the Jew the image and beat it and tormented it cruelly. Then happed a great marvel. For when the thieves disparted the goods, the holy Saint Nicholas, like as he had been in his array, appeared to the thieves and said to them. "Wherefore have I been beaten so cruelly for you and have so many torments. See how

my body is hewen and broken ; see how that the
red blood runneth down by my body. Go ye
fast and restore it again or else the ire of God
Almighty shall make you to be as one out of his
wit, and that all men shall know your felony and
that each of you shall be hanged." And they
said, "Who art thou that sayest to us such
things?" And he said to them, "I am Nicholas,
the servant of Jesus Christ, whom the Jew hath
so cruelly beaten for his goods that ye bare away."
Then they were afeard and came to the Jew and
heard what he had done to the image, and they
told him the miracle and delivered to him again
all his goods. And thus came the thieves to the
way of truth and the Jew to the way of Jesus
Christ.

A man for the love of his son that went to
school for to train, hallowed every year the feast
of Saint Nicholas much solemnly. On a time it
happed that the father had do make ready the
dinner and called many clerks to this dinner.
And the devil came to the gate in the habit of a
pilgrim for to demand alms. And the father anon
commanded his son that he should give alms to
the pilgrim. He followed him as he went for to
give him alms. And when he came to the cross-
way the devil caught the child and strangled him.
And when the father heard this he sorrowed
much and strongly wept, and bare the body into
his chamber. And began to cry for sorrow and
said, "Right sweet son, how is it with thee.
Saint Nicholas, is this the guerdon that ye have

A MIRACLE OF ST. NICHOLAS.

done to me because I have so long served you ?"
And as he said these words and other semblable,
the child opened his eyes and awoke like as he
had been asleep and arose up tofore all the people
and was raised from death to life by the prayers
of the blessed Saint Nicholas.

There was a rich man that by the merits of
Saint Nicholas had a son and called him, Deus
dedit, God gave.   And this rich man did do make
a chapel of Saint Nicholas in his dwelling-place
and did do hallow every year the feast of Saint
Nicholas.   And this manor was set by the land of
the Hagarenes paynims.   This child was taken
prisoner and deputed to serve the king.   The
year following, and the day that his father held
devoutly the feast of Saint Nicholas, the child
held a precious cup tofore the king, and remembered his taking, the sorrow of his friends, and
the joy that that day was made in the house of
his father, and began for to sigh sore high.   And
the king demanded him what him ailed, and the
cause of his sighing, and he told to him every
word wholly.   And when the king knew it he
said to him, "Whatsomever thy Nicholas do or
do not, thou shalt abide here with us."   And
suddenly there blew a much strong wind that
made all the house to tremble, and the child was
ravished, with the cup, and was set to fore the
gate where his father held the solemnity of Saint
Nicholas, in such wise that all they demeaned
great joy.   And some say that this child was of
Normandy and went over sea and was taken by

the Soldan which made him oft to be beaten to fore him. And as he was beaten on a Saint Nicholas day and was after set in prison, he prayed to Saint Nicholas as well for his beating that he suffered as for the great joy that he was wont to have on the day of Saint Nicholas. And when he had long prayed and sighed, he fell asleep. And when he awoke he found himself in the chapel of his father whereas was much joy made for him.

A noble man prayed to Saint Nicholas that he would by his merits get of Our Lord that he might have a son, and promised that he would bring his son to the church and would offer to him a cup of gold. Then the son was born and came to age. And the father commanded to make a cup, and the cup pleased him much and he retained it for himself and did do make another of the same value. And as they went sailing in a ship toward the church of Saint Nicholas, and as the child would have filled the cup, he fell into the water with the cup and anon was lost and came no more up. Yet nevertheless the father performed his vow, in weeping much tenderly for his son. And when he came to the altar of Saint Nicholas he offered the second cup. And when he had offered it, it fell down like as one had cast it under the altar. And he took it up and set it again upon the altar, and then it was cast further than tofore. And yet he took it up and remised it the third time upon the altar, and it was thrown again further than tofore. Of which thing all they that

were there marvelled, and men came for to see
this thing. And anon the child that had fallen
in the water in the sea came again all safe to fore
them all, and brought in his hands the first cup,
and recounted to the people that anon as he was
fallen in the sea the blessed Saint Nicholas came
and kept him that he had none harm. And thus
his father was glad, and offered to Saint Nicholas
both the two cups.

When there should be sung a new history of
Saint Nicholas in a church which was of the Holy
Cross and was subject to the Church of Our Lady
of Charity, the brethren prayed much instantly
their prior that they might sing this new history ;
which he in no wise would grant to them, and
said they ought not change their old for no new.
And yet the brethren prayed him more instantly,
and he in despite said, "Go your way, for in no
manner shall ye never have licence of me that
this new song shall be sung." And when the
feast of Saint Nicholas came, the brethren said
their matins all in heaviness and their vigils. And
when they were all in their beds, Saint Nicholas
appeared visibly and much fearfully to the prior
and drew him out by the hair, and smote him
down on the pavement of the dormitory, and began to sing the history, *O Pastor Eterne.* And at
every note he smote him with a rod that he held
in his hand right grievously on his back, and sang
melodiously this anthem unto the end. And then
the prior cried so loud that he awoke all his brethren and was borne to his bed as half dead. And

when he came to himself, he said, "Go ye and sing the new history of Saint Nicholas from henceforth."

XXVII.—SUNDRY MIRACLES OF OUR LADY.

W E read an example of a noble knight, which for to amend his life gave and rendered himself unto an abbey of Cistercians. And for as much as he was no clerk, there was assigned to him a master for to teach him, and he was to be with the brethren clerks. But he could no thing learn in long time that he was there save these two words, "Ave Maria," which words he had so sore imprinted in his heart that always he had them in his mouth where somever he was. At the last he died and was buried in the churchyard of the brethren. It happed after, that upon the tomb grew a right fair lily, and in every flower was written in letters of gold, Ave Maria. Of which miracle all the brethren were marvelled, and they did open the sepulchre, and found that the root of this lily came out of the mouth of the said knight. And anon they understood that Our Lord would have him honoured for the great devotion that he had to say these words Ave Maria.

Another knight there was, that had a fair place beside the high way where much people passed whom he robbed as much as he might, and so

used he his life.   But he had a good custom, for
every day he saluted the glorious Virgin Mary in
saying, "Ave Maria."   And for no labour he
left not to greet Our Lady as is said.   It happed
that an holy man passed by his house whom he
robbed and despoiled.   But the holy man prayed
them that robbed him that they would bring him
to their master, for he had to speak with him in
his house of a secret thing for his profit.   And
when the robbers heard that, they led him tofore
the knight their lord.   And anon the holy man
prayed him that he would do come all his meinie
tofore him.   And when his meinie by the commandment of the knight were assembled, the holy
man said, "Yet be they not all here.   There is
one yet to come."   Then one of them apperceived that the chamberlain of the lord was not
come.   And anon the knight make him to come.
And when the holy man saw him come, anon he
said, "I conjure thee by the virtue of Jesus
Christ our Lord thou say to us who thou art and for
what cause thou art come hither."   Anon the chamberlain answered, "Alas, now must I say and knowledge myself.   I am no man but am a devil in the
form of a man, and have taken it xii years, by
which space I have dwelled with this knight.   For
my master hath sent me hither to the end that I
should take heed night and day if this knight left
to say this salutation, Ave Maria.   For then I
should strangle him with mine own hands and
bring him to hell because of the evil life that he
hath led and leadeth.   But because he sayeth

A MIRACLE OF OUR LADY.

every day this salutation, Ave Maria, I might not
have him. And therefore I abode here so long,
for there passeth him no day but that he saluteth
Our Lady." When the knight heard this, he
was much afeard and fell down to the feet of this
holy man and demanded pardon of his sins. After
this the holy man said to the devil, "I command
thee in the name of Our Lord that thou depart
hence and go into another place where thou
mayest grieve nor annoy no man."

There was a knight much noble, and devout
unto our Lady which went to a tourneying. And
he found a monastery in his way which was of
the Virgin Mary, and entered in to it for to hear
mass. And there were masses one after another,
and for the honour of our Lady he would leave
none but that he heard them all. And when he
issued out of the monastery he hasted him apertly.
And they that returned from the tourney met
him, and said to him that he had ridden right
nobly. And they that hated him affirmed the
same, and all they together cried that he had
right nobly tourneyed : and some went to him
and said that he had taken them. Then he, that
was wise, avised him that the courteous virgin
and queen had so courteously honoured him, and
recounted all that was happened, and then returned he to the monastery, and ever after abode
in the service of Our Lord, the son of the blessed
Virgin.

There was a knight which was mighty and
rich that dispended foolishly his goods, and came

to so great poverty that he which had been
accustomed to give largely great things had need
to demand and ask the small. And he had a
right chaste wife and much devout to the blessed
Virgin Mary. And a great solemnity approached
at which the knight was accustomed to give many
gifts, and he had nothing to give, whereof he
was greatly ashamed. And he went into place
desert, full of heaviness and weeping, so long till
that the feast was passed, for to wail there his evil
fortune and for to eschew shame. And anon a
knight much horrible came sitting on a horse,
which areasoned the knight, and enquired of him
the cause of his great heaviness. And he told
him all by order as was happed to him. And
this foul knight said to him, "If thou wilt a
little obey to me, thou shalt abound in glory
and in riches more than thou wert tofore." And
he promised to the devil that he would do so
gladly if he accomplished that he promised. And
then he said to him, "Go home in to thine house,
and thou shalt find in such a place there so much
gold and so much silver. And thou shalt find
there also precious stones. And do so much that
such a day thou bring me hither thy wife." And
the knight returned home in to his house, and
found all things like as the devil had promised.
And anon he bought a palace, and gave great
gifts, and bought again his heritage, and took his
men again to him. And the day approached
when he had promised to lead his wife to the
fiend. And he called her, "Let us go to horse-

back, for ye must come with me unto a place far
hence." And she trembled and was afeard, and
durst not gainsay the commandment of her husband. And she commended herself devoutly to
the blessed Virgin Mary and began to ride after
her husband. And when they had ridden a good
while they saw in the way a church. And she
descended from the horse and entered in to the
church. Her husband abode without. And as
she commended her devoutly to the blessed Virgin
Mary in great devotion and contemplation, she
suddenly slept. And the glorious Virgin did on
semblable habit of this lady, and departed from
the altar, and issued out, and mounted upon the
horse. And the lady abode, sleeping in the
church, and the knight weened that she had been
his wife that was with him, and went alway
forth. And when he was come to the place assigned, the devil came with a great rush to the
place. And when he approached and came near,
he quaked and trembled anon, and durst not go
no nearer. Then said he to the knight. "Thou
most traitor of all men, wherefore hast thou deceived me, and hast rendered to me harm for such
great goods as I have given to thee ? I said to
thee that thou shouldst bring thy wife to me, and
thou hast brought the Mother of God. I would
have thy wife, and thou hast brought to me
Mary. For thy wife hath done to me many injuries wherefore I would take on her vengeance,
and thou hast brought to me this for to torment
me, and for to send me to hell." And when the

knight heard this he was sore abashed, and might not hold him from weeping, nor durst not speak for dread and marvel. And then the blessed Mary said, "Thou felon spirit, by what folly durst thou will to grieve and annoy my devout servant? This shall not be left in thee unpunished. I bind thee in this sentence that thou descend into hell, and that thou from henceforth have not presumption to grieve none that call upon me." And then he went away with great howling. And the man sprang down from his horse, and kneeled down on his knees to her feet. And the Virgin our Lady blamed him and commanded him to return again to his wife, which yet slept in the church, and bade him that he should cast away all the riches of the devil. And when he came again, he found his wife yet sleeping and awoke her, and told to her all that was befallen. And when they were come home, they threw away all the riches of the devil, and dwelled alway in the lovings of our Lady, and received afterwards many riches that our Lady gave to them.

XXVIII.—THE TRANSLATION OF SAINT MARK.

T happed in the year of grace iiii hundred xvi., in the time of Leo the Emperor, that the Venetians translated the body of Saint Mark from Alexandria to Venice in this manner. There were two merchants of Venice did so much, what by prayer and by their gifts, to two priests that kept the body of Saint Mark, that they suffered it to be borne secretly and privily unto their ships. And as they took it out of the tomb, there was so sweet an odour throughout all the city of Alexandria, that all the people marvelled, nor knew not from whence it came. Then the merchants brought it to the ship, and after hasted the mariners, and let the other ships have knowledge thereof. Then there was one man in another ship that japed and said, "Ween ye to carry away the body of Saint Mark? Nay, ye lead with you an Egyptian." Then anon after this word the ship wherein the holy body was turned lightly after him, and so rudely boarded the ship of him that had said that word that it brake one of the sides of the ship and would never leave it in peace till they had confessed that the body of Saint Mark was in the ship. That done she held her still.

Thus as they sailed fast they took none heed, and the air began to wax dark and thick, that they wist not where they were. Then appeared Saint Mark unto a monk, to whom the body of Saint Mark was delivered to keep, and bad him anon to strike their sails for they were nigh land. And he did so and anon they found land in an island. And by all the rivages where as they passed, it was said to them that they were well happy that they led so noble a treasure as the body of Saint Mark, and they prayed them that they would let them worship it. Yet there was a mariner that might not believe that it was the body of Saint Mark. But the devil entered into him and tormented him so long that he could not be delivered till he was brought to the holy body. And as soon as he confessed that it was the body of Saint Mark, he was delivered of the wicked spirit, and ever after he had great devotion to Saint Mark.

It happed after that the body of Saint Mark was closed in a pillar of marble, and right few people knew thereof by cause it should be secretly kept. Then it happed that they that knew thereof died, and there was none that knew where this great treasure might be. Wherefore the clerks and the lay people were greatly discomforted and wept for sorrow and doubted much that it had been stolen away. Then made they solemn processions and litanies and the people began to fast and be in prayers. And all suddenly the stones opened and shewed to all the people the place and stead where the holy body rested, then rendered they thankings to God of this that he had relieved them of their sorrow and anguish; and ordained that on that day they shall hold feast alway for this devout revelation.

There was a gentle man of Provence which had a servant that would fain go on pilgrimage to Saint Mark. But he could get no licence of his lord. At last he doubted not to anger his lord, but went thither much devoutly. And when his lord knew it, he bare it much greviously. And as soon as he was come again his lord commanded that his eyes should be put out. And the other servants that were ready to do the lord's will made ready sharp spikes of iron, and enforced them with all their power: and could not do it. Then commanded the lord to hew off his thighs with axes, but anon the iron was as soft as molten lead. Then commanded he to break his teeth with iron hammers, but the iron thereof was so soft that they could do him no harm. Then, when the lord saw the virtue of God so openly by the miracles of Saint Mark, he demanded pardon, and went to Venice to Saint Mark with his servant.

HERE was a bishop that led an holy and religious life, and loved Saint Andrew by great devotion, and worshipped him above all other saints, so that in all his works he remembered him every day and said certain prayers in the honour of God and Saint Andrew. In such wise that the enemy had envy on him, and set him for to deceive him with all his malice, and transformed him into the form of a right fair woman, and came to the palace of the bishop and said that she would be confessed to him. And the bishop bade her to go confess her to his penitencer. And she sent him word again that she would not shew the secrets of her confession to none but to him. And so the bishop commanded her to come, and she said to him, "Sir, I pray thee that thou have mercy on me, I am so as ye see in the years of my youth, and a maid, and was deliciously nourished from my infancy, and born of royal lineage; but I am come alone in strange habit, for my father which is a right mighty king would give me to a prince by marriage, whereto I answer that I have horror of all marriage, and I have given my virginity to Jesus Christ for ever. And in the end he constrained me so much that I must consent to his

will or suffer divers torments. So that I am fled
secretly away, and had liefer be in exile than to
break and corrupt my faith to my spouse. And
by cause I hear the praising of your right holy
life, I am fled unto you and to your guard, in hope
that I may find with you place of rest where as I
may be secret in contemplation, and eschew the
evil perils of this present life, and flee the divers
tribulations of the world." Of which thing the
bishop marvelled him greatly, as well for the great
nobleness of her lineage as for the beauty of her
body, for the burning of the great love of God,
and of the honest speaking of this woman. So
that the bishop answered to her with a meek and
pleasant voice: "Daughter, be sure and doubt
nothing. For He for whose love thou hast despised thyself and these things shall give to thee
great things. In this time present is little glory
or joy, but it shall be in time to come. And I
which am sergeant of the same, offer me to thee
and my goods: and choose thee an house where it
shall please thee. And I will that thou dine with
me this day." And she answered and said,
"Father, require of me no such thing, for by adventure some evil suspicion might come thereof.
And also the resplendour of your good renown
might be thereby impaired." To whom the
bishop answered, "We shall be many together,
and I shall not be with you alone, and therefore
there may be no suspicion of evil." Then they
came to the table and were set, that one against
that other, and the other folk here and there, and

the bishop entended much to her, and beheld her alway in the visage, and he marvelled of her great beauty. And thus as he fixed his eyes on her, his courage was hurt, and the ancient enemy saw the heart of him hurt with a grievous dart. And this devil apperceived it and began to increase her beauty more and more, in so much that the bishop was then ready for to require her to sin when he might.

Then a pilgrim came and began to smite strongly at the gate or door, and they would not open it. Then he cried and knocked more strongly, and the bishop axed of the woman if she would that the pilgrim should enter. And she said men should axe first of him a question, grievous enough, and if he could answer thereto he should be received, and if he could not he should abide without and not come in, as he that were not worthy but unweeting. And all agreed to her sentence, and enquired which of them were sufficient for to put the question. And when none was found sufficient, the bishop said, " None of us is so sufficient as ye, dame, for ye pass us all in fair speaking and shine in wisdom more than we all ; propose ye the question." Then she said, " Demand ye of him which is the greatest marvel that ever God made in little space ?" And then one went and demanded the pilgrim. The pilgrim answered to the messenger that it was the diversity and the excellency of the faces of men. For among all so many men as have been since the beginning of the world unto the end, two men might not be found of whom their faces were like and semblable in all things. And when the answer was heard, all they marvelled and said this was a very and right good answer of the question. Then the woman said, " Let the second question be proposed to him, which shall be more grievous to answer to, for to prove the better the wisdom of him." Which was this, " Whether the earth is higher than all the heaven?" And when it was demanded of him, the pilgrim answered, " In the heaven imperial where the body of Jesus Christ is, which is in the form of our flesh, He is more high than all the heaven." Of this answer they marvelled all when the messenger reported it, and praised marvellously his wisdom. Consequently she said the third question, which was more dark and grievous to assail. " For to prove the third time his wisdom, and that then he be worthy to be received at bishop's table, demand and axe of him how much space is from the abysm unto the same heaven?" Then the messenger demanded of the pilgrim, and he answered him, " Go to him that sent thee to me, and axe of him this thing. For he knoweth better than I and can better answer to it, for he hath measured this space when he fell from heaven into the abysm, and I never measured it. This is nothing a woman, but it is a devil which hath taken the form of a woman." And when the messenger heard this he was sore afeard and told tofore them all this that he had heard. And when the bishop heard this and all other, they were sore afeard, and anon forthwith the devil vanished away tofore their eyes. And after, the bishop came again to himself and reproved himself bitterly, weeping, repenting and requiring, pardon of his sin, and sent a messenger for to fetch and bring in the pilgrim, but he found him never after. Then the bishop assembled the people and told to them the manner of this thing, and prayed them that they all would be in orisons and prayers in such wise that Our Lord would shew to some person who this pilgrim was which had delivered him from so great peril. And then it was shewed that night to the bishop that it was Saint Andrew, which had put him in the habit of a pilgrim for the deliverance of him. Then began the bishop more and more to have devotion and remembrance to Saint Andrew than he had tofore.

AINT ANASTASIA had three damsels, which were sisters, that served her, whom she had enformed and taught that they should not reny their faith nor their good life for any menaces nor threatenings that the provost should do. The provost on a day came to them for to draw them to him. And Saint Anastasia did do hide them in her kitchen. The provost went after for to accomplish his ribaldry. And they kneeled down and prayed their prayers in such wise that the provost lost his wit. And when he supposed to have taken, embraced and holden them, he embraced pots, pans and cauldrons and kissed them. In such wise that he was so foul, horrible and black that when he issued out, his meinie that awaited his coming supposed that he had been out of his wit. And they beat him well, and after fled from him for fear and left him there alone. And he went for to complain him unto the Emperor. And when he came to the gate, the sergeants that saw him so black and smutted, beat him well with rods, and scratched him in the visage, and held him for wood. And the caitiff knew not that he was so foul and black, and therefore he marvelled much more why they did to him so much shame when tofore they did to him so much honour. And he had supposed that he had been clad in a white robe. When they told him how he was arrayed, then he supposed that the maidens had enchanted him and sent for them and would have despoiled them all naked before him. But their clothes were anon so fast glued to their bodies that in no wise they might be taken off nor despoiled. And then he fell asleep and so fast that no man might awake him. At the last these virgins were martyred and suffered death.

XXXI.—A VISION OF SAINT JOHN THE ALMONER.

SAINT JOHN the Almoner was Patriarch of Jerusalem. He saw on a time, in a vision, a much fair maid which had on her head a crown of olive, and when he saw her he was greatly abashed and demanded her what she was. This maid answered to him, " I am Mercy which brought from heaven the Son of God. If thou wilt wed me thou shalt fare the better." Then he, understanding that the olive betokeneth mercy, began that same day to be merciful, in such wise that he was called almoner and he called alway the poor people his lord.

O N a time as Saint Anthony wasl in wilderness in his prayer and was weary, he said to Our Lord, "Lord, I have great desire to be saved, but my thoughts let me." Then appeared an angel to him and said, "Do as I do and thou shalt be safe." And he went out and saw him one while labour, and another while pray. Do this and thou shalt be saved.

XXXIII.—SAINT BERNARD AND THE VILLEIN.

I N a time Saint Bernard rode upon an horse by the way, and met a villein by the way. And he said to the villein that he had not his heart firm and stable in praying. And the villein or up-landish man had great despite thereof, and said that he had his heart firm and stable in all his prayers. And Saint Bernard, which would vanquish him and shew his folly, said to him, "Depart a little from me, and begin thy *Paternoster* in the best intent thou canst. And if thou canst finish it without thinking on any other thing, without doubt I shall give to thee the horse that I am on. And thou shalt promise to me, by thy faith, that if thou think on any other thing, thou shalt not hide it from me." And the man was glad, and reputed the horse his, and granted it him. And he went apart and began his *Paternoster*. And he had not said the half when he wondered if he should have the saddle withal. And therewith he returned to Saint Bernard and said that he had thought in praying. And after that he had no more will to advance him.

XXXIV.—THE HERMIT AND SAINT GREGORY.

IN that time there was an hermit, an holy man, which had left and forsaken all the goods of the world for God's sake, and had retained nothing but a cat with which he played oft, and held it in his lap deliciously. On a day it happed that he prayed God devoutly that He should vouchsafe to shew to him to what saint he would be in like joy in heaven, because for His love he had left all the world and renounced it. Upon this God shewed him in a vision that Saint Gregory and he should have like joy in heaven. And when he understood this, he sighed sore and praised little his poverty which he had long suffered and borne, if he should have like merit which abounded so greatly in secular riches. Upon this came a voice to him which said that the possession maketh not a man in this world rich, but the ardour of covetise. "Then be still thou: darest thou compare thy poverty to the riches of Saint Gregory, which lovest more thy cat, with whom thou ceasest not to stroke and play than Saint Gregory doth all his riches, for he ceaseth never to give alms for

God's sake?" Then the hermit thanked Almighty God, and prayed that he might have his merit and reward with Saint Gregory in the glory of Paradise.

XXXV.—THE PARENTS OF
SAINT THOMAS OF CANTERBURY.

ILBERT BECKET was a burgess of the city of London and he was a good devout man and took the cross upon him and went on pilgrimage to the Holy Land, and had a servant with him. And when he had accomplished his pilgrimage, he was taken homeward by the heathen men and brought into the prison of a prince named Amerant, where long time he and his fellowship suffered much pain and sorrow. And the prince had great affection towards this Gilbert and had oft communication with him of the Christian faith and of the realm of England. By which conversation it fortuned that the daughter of this prince had especial love unto this Gilbert and was familiar with him. And on a time she disclosed her love to him saying, if he would promise to wed her, she would forsake friends, heritage and country for his love and become Christian. And after long communication between them, he promised to wed her if she would become Christian, and told to her the place of his dwelling in England. And after, by the purveyance of God, the said Gilbert escaped and came home. And after this it fortuned so that this prince's daughter stole

privily away, and passed many a wild place and
great adventure, and by God's purveyance at the
last came in to London, demanding and crying,
"Becket, Becket," for more English could she
not. Wherefore the people drew about her (what
for the strange array of her as for they understood her not), and many a shrewd boy. So long
she went till she come to fore Gilbert's door.
And as she there stood, the servant that had been
with Gilbert in prison, which was named Richard,
saw her and knew anon that it was the prince's
daughter. And he went in to his master and told
him how this maid stood at his door, and anon he
went out to see her. And as soon as she saw him,
she fell in a swoon for joy. And Gilbert took
her up and comforted her and brought her into
his house : and soon went to the bishops which
then were six at Paul's and rehearsed all the matter. And after, they christened her, and forthwith wedded her to Gilbert Becket ; and within
time reasonable and accustomed was brought
forth between them a fair son named Thomas.

There was a lady in England that desired
greatly to have grey eyes, for she had a conceit
she should be the more beauteous in the sight of
the people. And only for that cause she made a
vow for to visit Saint Thomas upon her bare feet.
And when she came thither and had devoutly
made her prayers to have her desire, suddenly she
was stark blind. And then she perceived that
she had offended and displeased Our Lord in the

request and cried God mercy of the offence, and besought Him full meekly to be restored to her sight again. And by the merits of the blessed Saint Thomas she was restored to her sight again and was glad to have her old eyes and returned home again and lived holily to her life's end.

There was a tame bird kept in a cage which was learned to speak. And on a time he fled out of the cage and flew in to the field. And there came a sparrowhawk and would have taken this bird and pursued after. And the bird, being in great dread, cried, saying, "Saint Thomas, help me," like as he had heard other speak; and the sparrowhawk fell down dead and the bird escaped harmless.

XXXVI.—MIRACLES OF SAINT AUSTIN OF CANTERBURY.

A S Saint Austin came into Oxford-shire to a town that is called Compton, to preach the word of God, to him the curate said, "Holy father, the lord of this lordship hath been ofttimes warned of me to pay his tithes to God and yet he with-holdeth them. And therefore I have cursed him, and I find him the more obstinate." To whom Saint Austin said, "Son, why payest thou not thy tithes to God and to the church? Knowest thou not that the tithes be not thine but belongen to God?" And then the knight said to him, "I know well that I till the ground, wherefore I ought as well to have the tenth sheaf as the ix." And when Saint Austin could not turn the knight's intent, then he departed from him and went to mass. And or he began, he charged that all they that were accursed should go out of the church. And then rose a dead body and went out into the church yard with a white cloth on his head, and stood still there till the mass was done. And then Saint Austin went to him and demanded him what he was, and he answered and said, "I was sometime lord of this town, and be-cause I would not pay my tithes to my curate he accursed me, and so I died and went to hell."

And then Saint Austin bade him bring him to
the place where his curate was buried, and then
the carrion brought him thither to the grave.
And by cause that all men should know that life
and death be in the power of God, Saint Austin
said, "I command thee in the name of God to
arise for we have need of thee." And then he
arose anon and stood before all the people. To
whom Saint Austin said, "Thou knowest well
that Our Lord is merciful, and I demand thee
brother, if thou knowest this man." And he
said, "Yea, would God that I had never known
him. For he was a with-holder of his tithes and
in all his life an evil-doer. Thou knowest that
Our Lord is merciful, and as long as the pains
of hell endure let us also be merciful to all
Christians." And then Saint Austin delivered to
the curate a rod, and there the knight kneeling
on his knees was assoiled. And then he commanded him to go again to his grave; and he
entered anon in to his grave and forthwith fell to
ashes and powder. And then Saint Austin said
to the priest, "How long hast thou lain here?"
And he said, "An hundred and fifty year." And
then he asked how it stood with him and he
said, "Well, holy father, for I am in everlasting
bliss." And then said Saint Austin, "Wilt thou
that I pray to Almighty God that thou abide here
with us to confirm the hearts of men in very
belief?" And then he said, "Nay, holy father,
for I am in a place of rest." And then said
Saint Austin, "Go in peace and pray for me and

for all holy church." And he then entered again in to his grave and anon the body was turned into earth. Of this sight the lord was sore afeard and came all quaking to Saint Austin and to his curate, and demanded forgiveness of his trespass and promised to make amends, and ever after to pay his tithes and to follow the doctrine of Saint Austin.

After this Saint Austin entered into Dorsetshire, and came in to a town where as were wicked people that refused his doctrine and preaching utterly, and drove him out of the town casting on him the tails of thornback or like fishes. Wherefore he besought Almighty God to shew His judgment on them. And God sent to them a shameful token, for the children that were born after in that place had tails, as it is said, till they had repented them. It is said commonly that this fell at Stroud in Kent, but, blessed be God, at this day is no such deformity.

Also in the same country was a young man that was lame, dumb and deaf, and by the prayers of Saint Austin he was made whole. And then soon after he was dissolute and wanton and noyed and grieved the people with jangling and talking in the church. And then God sent to him his old infirmity again because of his misguiding. And at the last he fell to repentance and asked God forgiveness and Saint Austin. And Saint Austin prayed for him, and he was made whole again the second time. And after that he continued in good and virtuous living to his life's end.

XXXVII.—A PRIEST ESPOUSED TO
SAINT AGNES.

I T is read that when the church of Saint Agnes was void, the pope said to a priest that he would give to him a wife for to nourish and keep : and he meant to commise the church of Saint Agnes to his cure. And he delivered to him a ring and bade him to wed the image. And the image put forth her finger and he set on it the ring, and anon she closed the finger to her hand and kept the ring. And so he spoused her.

XXXVIII.—A MIRACLE OF SAINT JAMES THE GREAT.

A MERCHANT was detained of a tyrant, and, all despoiled, was wrongfully put in prison. And he called much devoutly Saint James in to his help. And Saint James appeared to him tofore them that kept him, and they awoke; and he brought him unto the highest of the tower and anon the tower bowed down so low that the top was even with the ground. And he went out without leaping and unbound of his irons. Then his keepers followed after, but they had no power to see him.

XXXIX.—A MIRACLE OF SAINT GENEVIEVE.

IN the time that the city of Paris was assieged by the term of ten years, like as the ancient histories rehearse, there followed so great famine and hunger that many died for hunger. The holy virgin, that pity constrained her, went to the Seine for to go fetch by ship some victuals. When she came unto a place of Seine where as of custom ships were wont to perish, she made the ship to be drawn to the rivage and commanded to cut down a tree that was in the water, and she set her to prayer. Then as the ships would have smitten upon the tree, it fell down, and two wild heads, grey and horrible, issued thereout which stank so sore that the people there were envenomed by the space of two hours. And never after perished ship there, thank be to God and His holy saint.

XL.—THE DEVIL APPEARS TO SAINT MARTIN.

T happed on a day that the devil appeared to Saint Martin in the form of a king, in purple and a crown on his head, with hose and shoon gilt, with an amiable mouth and glad cheer and visage. And when they were both still awhile, the devil said, " Martin, knowest thou not He whom thou worshippest? I am Christ that am descended into earth and will first shew me to thee." And as Saint Martin, all admarvelled, said no thing, yet the devil said to him, " Wherefore doubtest thou Martin to believe me, when thou seest that I am Christ?" And then Martin blessed of the Holy Ghost, said, " Our Lord Jesus Christ saith not that He shall come in purple nor with a crown resplendishing. I shall never believe that Jesus Christ shall come but if it be in habit and form such as He suffered death in, and that the sign of the cross be borne to fore Him." And with that word the devil vanished away and all the hall was filled with stench.

XLI.—THE DEVIL APPEARS TO SAINT DUNSTAN.

N a time as Saint Dunstan sat at his work, his heart was on Jesus Christ, his mouth occupied with holy prayers, and his hands busy on his work. But the devil, which ever had great envy at him, came to him in an eventide in the likeness of a woman, as he was busy to make a chalice, and with smiling said that she had great things to tell him. And then he bade her say what she would. And then she began to tell him many nice trifles and no manner virtue therein. And then he supposed that she was a wicked spirit, and anon caught her by the nose with a pair of tongs of iron burning hot. Then the devil began to roar and cry and fast drew away : but Saint Dunstan held fast till it was far within the night and then let her go. And the fiend departed with an horrible noise and cry, and said that all the people might hear, "Alas what shame hath this carle done to me, how may I best quit him again ? " But never after the devil had never lust to tempt him in that craft.

HERE was a knight that lay dead and his spirit taken from him, and a while after the soul returned to the body again.   And what he had seen done he told, and said, There was a bridge, and under hat bridge was a flood, foul, horrible and full of tench; and on that other side of the bridge was meadow, sweet, odorant and adorned full of all nanner flowers.   And there on that side of the ridge were peoples assembled clad all in white, hat were filled with the sweet odour of the lowers.   And the bridge was such, that if any f the unjust would pass over the bridge, he hould slide and fall into that stinking river, and he righteous people passed over lightly and urely into that delectable place.   And this night saw there a man named Peter which lay ound, and great weight of iron upon him. Which when he axed why he lay so there, it was aid to him of another, "He suffereth by cause if ny man were delivered to him to do vengeance, e desired more to do it by cruelty than by bedience."   Also he said he saw there a pilgrim, hat, when he came to the bridge, passed over ith great lightness and shortly, by cause he had ell lived here and purely in the world and

without sin. And he saw there another named
Stephen, which, when he would have passed, his
feet slipped that he fell half over the bridge.
And then there came some horrible black men
and did all that they might do to draw him down
by the legs: and then came other right fair
creatures and white, and took him by the arms
and drew him up. And as this strife endured,
this knight that saw these things, returned to his
body and knew not which of them vanquished.
But this way we understand that the wicked
deeds that he had done strove against the works
of alms, for by them that drew him by the arms
upward, it appeared that he loved alms, and by
the other, that he had not perfectly lived against
the sins of the flesh.

It is read that some fishers of Saint Thibault,
that fished on a time in harvest took a great piece
of ice instead of a fish. And they were gladder
thereof than of a fish, by cause the bishop had a
great burning of heat in his leg, and they laid
that ice thereto and it refreshed him much. And
on a time the bishop heard the voice of a man in
the ice, and he conjured him to tell him what he
was. And the voice said to him, "I am a soul
which for my sins am tormented in this ice, and
may be delivered if thou say for me thirty masses
continually together in thirty days." And the
bishop emprised to say them, and when he had
said half of them he made ready to continue
forth and say the other. And the devil made
a dissension in the city that the people of the

city fought each against other, and then the
bishop was called for to appease this discord,
and did off his vestments and left to say the mass.
And on the morn he began all new again, and
when he had said the two parts, him seemed that
a great host had beseiged the city, so that he was
constrained by dread, and left to say the office of
the mass. And after yet, he began again service,
and when he had all accomplished except the last
mass, which he would have begun, all the town
and the bishop's house was taken by fire. And
when his servants came to him and bad him
leave his mass, he said, "Though all the city
should be burnt, I shall not leave to say the
mass." And when the mass was done the ice
was molten, and the fire that they had supposed
to have seen, was but a phantasm and did no
harm.

There was a man that alway as he passed
through the churchyard, he said, "De profundis"
for all christian souls. And on a time he was
beset with his enemies, so that for succour he
leapt in to the churchyard. And they followed
for to have slain him; and anon all the dead
bodies arose, and each held such an instrument in
his hand that they defended him that prayed for
them, and chased away his enemies, putting them
in great fear.

It is read in the book of the miracles of our
blessed lady Saint Mary, that a judge named
Stephen was at Rome, and took gladly gifts and
perverted the judgments. And this judge took

away by force three houses that were longing to the church of Saint Lawrence and a garden of Saint Agnes and possessed them wrongfully. It happed that the judge died and was brought to judgment to fore God. And when Saint Lawrence saw him, he went to him in great despite and strained him three times by the arm right hard and tormented him by great pain. And Saint Agnes and other virgins deigned not to look on him but turned their visages away from him. And then the judge giving sentence against him, said, " By cause he hath withdrawn other men's things, and hath taken gifts and sold truth, that he should be put in the place of Judas the traitor." And Saint Projectus whom the said Stephen had much loved in his life came to the blessed Lawrence and to Saint Agnes and cried them mercy for him. Then the blessed Virgin Mary and they prayed to God for him. And then it was granted to them that the soul of him should go again to the body, and there should do his penance thirty days. And our blessed Lady commanded him, that as long as he lived he should say the psalm, *Beati immaculati.* And when the soul came to the body again, his arm was like as it had been burnt, like as he had suffered that hurt in his body, and that token and sign was in him as long as he lived. Then rendered he that which he had taken and did his penance. And at xxx day he passed out of this world to Our Lord.

I N a time as Saint Patrick preached in Ireland the faith of Jesus Christ, he had but little profit by his predication for he could not convert the evil, rude and wild people. And he prayed to Our Lord Jesus Christ that He would shew them some sign openly, fearful and ghastful, by which they might be converted and be repentant of their sins. Then, by the commandment of God, Saint Patrick made in the earth a great circle with his staff, and anon the earth, after the quantity of the circle, opened and there appeared a great pit and a deep. And Saint Patrick, by the revelation of God, understood that there was a place of purgatory into which whomever entered therein, he should never have other penance nor feel none other pain ; and there was shewed to him that many should enter which should never return nor come again. And they that should return should abide but from one morn to another and no more. And many entered that came not again. As touching this pit or hole, which is named Saint Patrick's Purgatory, some hold opinion that the second Patrick, which was an abbot and no bishop, that God shewed to him his place of purgatory. But certainly such a place there is in Ireland, wherein many men have been and yet daily go in and come again. And some have had there many marvellous visions and seen grisly and horrible pains. Of whom there be books made as of Tundale and other.

HERE was a man that had a devil within him, and after went to Milan, and anon as he entered the city the devil left him. And as soon as he went out of the city the devil re-entered in him again. hen he demanded him why he did so, and he swered by cause he was afeared of Ambrose.

There was a maid demanded drink of a servant her father's. And she gave her drink and said, The devil mote thou drink." And she drank, d her seemed that fire entered into her body. hen began she to cry and her belly to swell like a barrel, so that each man saw that she was deoniac. And she was two years in that estate d after was brought to the tomb of Saint Eliza-:th and was made perfectly whole and delivered the fiend.

There was a man called Roba which had lost s gown and all the money that he had. When came into his house and saw himself in so great verty he lay upon his bed and called the devils d gave himself to them. Then came to him ree devils which cast down Roba upon the floor his bed-chamber, and took him by the neck : d it seemed that they would have strangled him in such wise that he unneth might speak. When they that were in the house beneath heard him cry, they went to him; but the devils said to them that they should return, and they supposed that Roba had said so, and returned. And after anon he began to cry again, then apperceived they well that they were the devils, and fetched the priest, which conjured in the name of Saint Peter the devils that they should go their way: then two of them went away and the third abode. And his friends brought Roba on the morning to the church of the friars. Then there came a friar named William of Vercello, and this friar William demanded what was his name, and the fiend answered, "I am called Balcefas." Then the friar commanded that he should go out. And anon the fiend called him by his name as he had known him and said, "William, William, I shall not go out for thee, for he is ours and hath given himself to us." Then he conjured him in the name of Saint Peter the martyr. And then anon he went his way, and the man was all whole, and took penance for his trespass and was after a good man.

As Saint Dominic preached on a time, some ladies that had been deceived of heretics kneeled at his feet and said to him, "Servant of God, help us. If it be true that thou preachest, the spirit of error hath blinded our minds. And he said, "Be ye firm, and tarry a little, and ye shall see what lord ye have served." And anon they saw spring out of the middle of them a cat right horrible, which was more than a great dog, and had great

eyes and flaming, her tail long, broad and bloody.
She had the tail raised on high, and shewed the
after end which way she turned him, out of which
issued a terrible stench. And when she had turned
hither and thither among the ladies, at the last she
mounted up by the bell rope in to the steeple, and
vanished away, leaving a great stench after her.
And the ladies thanked God and were converted
to the faith Catholic.

NOTES.

P. 4.   St. Agnes.

January 21st.   Martyred A.D. 304 during the Diocletian persecution.

P. 11.   St. Alban.

June 17th.   This account of the first recorded martyrdom in Britain is in the collection of " frere John of Benynguay." It very closely coincides with a poem by John Lydgate written in 1439, and produced at the request of John Wheathamstede, Abbot of St. Alban's, who caused a copy to be illuminated and hung up over the altar of the abbey church.   Robert Catton, abbot, had it printed by John Herford of St. Albans in 1534—four years before the dissolution of the monastery. The title-page reads thus :—" Here begynnethe ye glorious lyfe and passion of Seint Albon prothomartyr of Englande, and also the lyfe and passion of Saint Amphabel, which converted Saint Albon to the fayth of Christe."

P. 27.   St. Barlaam and St. Josaphat.

There is no greater surprise in hagiology than this fantastic Oriental legend, which contains a number of tales from Indian folk-lore and is founded on the life of Buddha.   It's Greek form belongs to the seventh or eighth century and has usually been ascribed to St. John of Damascus, at one time chief councillor or vizier to the Caliph of Damascus and afterwards a monk of St. Sabas near Jerusalem.   The foremost theologian of his age he especially distinguished himself by defending in controversy the sacred images against the Iconoclastic assaults of the Emperor Leo the Isaurian and his son Constantine Copronymus.   He died about A.D. 736.   His

authorship of the legend has been called in question by recent
authorities especially by Zotenberg. (Notice sur le livre de
Barlaam et Joasaph, Paris, 1886). Whoever was the writer he
obtained his information as he says from " pious men from a
distant district of Ethiopia called India." The earlier part
of the story follows in its main outlines the legendary life of
Buddha as contained in *Lalita Vistara*, the " Diffusion of Joys."
The date of that book—which is not, by the way, in the
Buddhistic canon—is uncertain, but its substance was certainly known three centuries before the appearance of the tale of
Barlaam and Josaphat. The very name of the hero is the
same. " Josaphat is only the Roman spelling for Yosaphat,
this again being a confusion between the Biblical Jehoshaphat
and the Greek form Joasaph. This is distinctly derived
from the Arabic ; it is a contracted form of Yodasaph, which
is a mis-reading for Bodasaph, since y and b in Arabic are
only distinguished by a diacritical point. Bodasaph is directly
derived, through the Pehlevi, from Bodhisattva, the technical
title of the man who is destined to attain Buddhahood, a
description which exactly applies to the career of Josaphat."
(*Barlaam and Josaphat.* Ed. by J. Jacobs, D. Nutt, 1895.
Introd. p. xlvii.) The *Lalita Vistara* tells how a king of
the Sakyas in North-East India was informed that his newly-
born son Siddhartha would either be a great conqueror or the
Buddha and an ascetic. To avoid the latter alternative he
shuts him up in a palace where only pleasant sights could
meet his eyes. Then follow the Four Signs or Visions
which lead the Buddha to renounce the world.—
  'Now Bhikshu the Bodhisattva ordered the charioteer,
"Quickly get the chariot ready ; I propose to go to the
garden."
  Thereupon the charioteer repaired to the King S'uddhod-
ana, and said, " Sire the Prince desires to go to the garden."
  The king reflected. The prince has never been to the
pleasure-garden to behold its well-laid parterres except in my
company. Now if he should go there surrounded by ladies
he will be disposed to dalliance and not think of renouncing
his home. So, out of profuse affection for the Bodhisattva,
he caused the news to be published by the ringing of bells
throughout the town that on the seventh day the Prince

would proceed to the pleasure-garden to behold the grounds ;
therefore the people should hide all offensive objects so that
the prince might not see anything repulsive ; but all pleasant
and auspicious sights should be put forward.

Now on the seventh day the whole town was decorated.
The garden was spread with flowers of various colours, and
parasols, standards, and flags were set up everywhere. The
road by which the Bodhisattva would proceed was watered,
smoothed, sprinkled with perfumes, scattered with flowers,
made redolent with the incense of pastilles, and set off with
pitchers of water and rows of plantain trees : many-coloured
awnings were hung up everywhere, and also net-works decorated with jewelled bells and garlands. The four-fold army
was set in array and attendants were ready for the decoration
of the prince's apartments.

The prince started for the garden by the eastern gate,
attended by a large retinue. Now, through the grace of the
Bodhisattva and the device of the Devaputras of the class
Súddhávásakáyika, there appeared in front of that road an
emaciated old decrepit person ; his body was covered with
prominent veins ; he was toothless, covered with flabby ten-
dons, and grey-haired ; he was humped ; his mouth was
sunken ; he was broken down, diseased, and leaning on a
staff. He had long passed his youth ; there was a rattling
cough in his throat ; bent forward by the weight of his body
he was leaning on a staff with the weight of his body and
members.

Though he knew what the sight meant, the Boddhisattva
thus questioned the charioteer :

"Who is this weak, powerless man, with dried-up flesh,
blood and skin, prominent veins, whitened head, scattered
teeth and emaciated body, painfully tottering on, leaning on
a staff ? "

The Charioteer replied :

"Lord, this is a person over-powered by age, his organs
are feeble, and his strength and vigour are gone. Abandoned
by his friends, he is helpless and unfit for work like wood
left alone in a forest."

The Boddhisattva said :

"Explain, charioteer, if this be the peculiarity of his tribe, or is it the condition of the whole world? Quickly answer this question according to fact, so that I may, on hearing it, enquire about it's source."

The charioteer replied:

" Lord, this is not a peculiarity of his race or country. Age wears out youth in the whole creation. Even thou shalt be separated from the society of thy mother and father and kinsmen and relatives. There is no other lot for man."

The Boddhisattva said:

"Condemnable truly, charioteer, are the ignorant and youthful, who, in the pride and intoxication of their youth, do not reflect on decay. Turn back the chariot, I do not wish to see anything farther. Of what avail are pleasures and enjoyments to me when I am subject to decay?"

Then the Boddhisattva caused the chariot to be turned back and entered the palace.' (From the *Lalita Vistara*, translated by Rájendralála Mitra, Calcutta, 1848.)

Afterwards he met a sick man, then a dead man in his shroud, followed by his kinsmen crying, weeping and moaning, and finally his choice of the ascetic life was determined by the sight of a calm, quiet self-possessed Bhikshu, devoid of affection and enmity, who had renounced all sensuous desires. In the Christian legend this last has become Barlaam the hermit.

The transmigrations of the story are traced in Mr. Jacob's Introduction. When it took it's place among the chronicles of the saints, it was used as a means of presenting in a palatable form the principal doctrines of Christianity. The Greek narrator puts bodily into the mouth of Nachor, the unwilling defender of the faith, the whole of a celebrated document which was supposed to be lost till it was discovered here, the Apology of Aristides, presented to the Emperor Hadrian in the first half of the second century. (*The Apology of Aristides*, Cambridge Texts and Studies, Vol. I., 1891.)

The text in the *Golden Legend* is very much shorter than the original: the Latin version made in the eleventh or twelfth century was abridged by Vincent de Beauvais, whose narrative furnished the matter for Jacobus de Voragine's still more scanty reproduction. Some of the apologues are omitted. It was these of course which secured for the legend

such ready acceptance that before the thirteenth century it
was translated into almost every known language of the
world. Some of them found their way into other collections,
especially into the Gesta Romanorum, originally a "Preacher's
Promptuary of Anecdote" and then a well-known storehouse of poetic materials : doubtless the tale of the caskets
was known to Shakespeare through its presence there. Barlaam and Josaphat were included in the "Catalogus Sanctorum" of Petrus de Natalibus (about 1370) and in the
revised Martyrology sanctioned by Gregory XIII. (1584).
In the Eastern church Josaphat alone is honoured on August
26th, but in the West the 27th of November is assigned to
both saints.

"Buddha has become a Saint of the Roman church;
though under a different name the sage of Kapilavastu, the
founder of a religion which, whatever we may think of it's
dogma, is, in the purity of it's morals, nearer to Christianity
than any other religion, and which counts even now, after an
existence of 2,400 years, more believers than any other creed,
has received the highest honours that the Christian church
can bestow." (Max Müller, Selected Essays I. p. 546.)

P. 52.   St. Brendan, abbot.

Brandon or Brendan—named otherwise Brandan, Brennan,
Broenfind or Brennain—son of Finnlug, was born in Ireland
near Tralee and descended from Ciar, the ancestor of the
Ciarraighe whose name survives in that of County Kerry.
The date of his birth is given as about the year 484. His
youth was spent in intercourse with saints who at that time
abounded in Ireland, and when' he arrived at man's estate he
devoted himself to the religious life. The seas were no bar-
rier between members of the community of Celtic monks,
and Brendan, like many others, visited his brethren in distant
countries in Wales and Brittany, and is said, though doubt-
fully, to have been a pupil of St. Gildas. He founded monasteries, one at Ardfert and another at Cluain-fearta or
Clonfert—that is Cluain-fearta-Brennain, Lawn of the grave
of Brendan—which became a renowned abbey of which there
are remains to this day. Three thousand monks, so it is

said, gathered round him there. In his old age he paid a visit to St. Columb of the Cells at Iona. Brendan had reached his ninety-fifth year when he died. The day which the calendars assign for his commemoration is May 16th.

The tradition of St. Brendan's voyage reaches back to within a hundred years of his life-time; and a church festival founded on it, Egressio familiae Brendani, the departure of the following of Brendan, is of early date. Some genuine incident very probably gave rise to the legend. Irish monks of the fifth and sixth centuries were often hardy seamen: moved by the love of solitude and the desire of penetrating the unknown, they wandered far over the western seas in frail coaches of wicker-work and hide; and in such ill-provided hazardous journeying the herbage of each new-discovered islet would be green and various beyond the use of nature and its springs of water more delicious than any nectar. A voyage to the Hebrides or the Orkneys—perhaps to St. Kilda's island where a ruined chapel of St. Brendan now stands—might be sufficient to sow the seed of a legend. Some will have it that the saintly rover was carried to shores which deserve a rapturous description, perhaps even to America which the Vikings also were to reach. But what St. Brendan did and what he saw cannot now be accurately known: his voyage, as we have it, is a mosaic of tales of the sea gathered from many different sources.

The earliest account is contained in the life of his disciple, St. Malo, written by Bili, deacon of Aleth—afterwards St. Malo—towards the end of the ninth century. Malo, or Machu—Machutus is the Latin form—persuades his master Brendan to set forth with him in search of Yma, the Island of the Blest. On their first voyage they sail round the Orkneys and return home. A second time they make the attempt. On the day of Easter, St. Malo desires to celebrate Mass. He casts his eyes around but sees no fit place, only the sky above and the water beneath. So he prays to God and a whale rises up in the water; some fear, but Malo bids them be of good courage, and he goes and celebrates Mass on the whale's back, and when all have returned, the monster sinks down again into the depths of the sea. Then they come to an island where is a huge barrow. St. Malo prays and it's inmate, a man of incomparable stature, is raised from the dead. The giant, once a pagan and idolater, beseeches the saint to baptize him that he may be delivered from hell. His request is granted; and in return, he takes up the ship's anchor and walking on the bottom of the sea, guides them towards the place they seek. But great tempests arise, they return to the giant's island and there he dies and is devoutly buried. They wander for seven years, but never find the Island of the Blest.

Two very early notices of St. Brendan also contain some mention of the whale; apparently they make the saint perform the whole of his journey on the creature's back. A poet, Cuimin of Connor who died in the sixth century writes:

> " Brendan loved perpetual mortification,
> According to his synod and his flock:
> Seven years he spent on the great whale's back;
> It was a distressing mode of mortification."

In the life of St. David (Acta Sanctorum May I. p. 44) St. Barrius riding on a horse amid the waves meets with St. Brendan who is leading a marvellous life on the whale's back.

The completed legend of St. Brendan owes much, as it appears, to a tradition of a similar undertaking by a Celtic hero, namely Maelduin, whose *Imrama* were part of the necessary equipment of an Irish bard. The present text of Maelduin's voyage is not earlier than the eleventh century. But Zimmer (Brendans Meerfahrt in *Zeitschrift für Deutsches Alterthum*, vol. xxxiii., Berlin 1889) asserts that it is founded on a pre-Christian legend from which much in St. Brendan's Voyage has been borrowed. Another possible source has been suggested in Sindbad's adventures in the Thousand and One Nights. (For a full comparison see M. J. de Goeje *La Légende de Saint Brandan*, Leyden, 1890.) This mosaic of sea-tales contained however much that was the common property of East and West and it would perhaps be difficult to extablish any direct connexion between the two narratives.

An Irish version of St. Brendan's life is contained in the *Lives of Saints from the Book of Lismore.* (Edited by Whitley Stokes, LL.D., Anecdota Oxoniensia, Clarendon Press.)

The fame of St. Brendan was due to the Latin "Navigatio" which appeared on the Continent in the eleventh century, probably first on the banks of the Rhine whither many monks from Ireland had been driven by the invasions of the Danes in the eighth and ninth centuries. It was surely well deserved. There is nothing in literature quite like this fairy-tale of the cloister, this dream of the world seen through the medium of the monastic imagination. "Le poëme de Saint Brandon" Renan calls it, "une de plus étonnantes créations de l'ésprit humain."

The "monkish Odyssey" became the most popular of medieval tales. During the two hundred years which followed it's appearance in Latin, it was translated into German, French, English and Spanish. Troubadours made it a theme for verse, one of them at the bidding of a Queen, Adelaide of Louvain, wife of Henry I. England has no less than thirty-seven manuscripts of different versions and there are eleven in the Bibliothéque Nationale in Paris. Commentators reckon the "Navigatio" among the sources of Dante's Divine Comedy.

Two old-world traditions are blended in the object of St. Brendan's voyage : it is at once the Garden of Eden, supposed to be still in unaltered existence on the earth, and also the Fortunate Island of the West, the Garden of the Hesperides, the Ogygia of Calypso, in it's Celtic form Hy Brasail, the Island of the Blest. Baring-Gould's *Curious Myths of the Middle Ages* deals copiously with both. His remarks as to the Terrestrial Paradise may be supplemented by the following extracts from Bartholomew de Glanvilla, whose book, *De Proprietatibus Rerum*, written about 1248, was for a long time a favourite cyclopaedia of useful knowledge. Paradise is included in the description of the countries of the world, placed in an alphabetical arrangemen between the Orkneys and Parthia :

"God from the beginning ordained and arrayed a place of liking with herbs and trees, and in the beginning of the world, that is in the East : and that place is most merry and far in space of land and sea out of the country that we dwell in. And it is so high that it reacheth almost to the circle of the moon ; where also by reason of the height the waters of the great flood could not come. The trees wither not nor their leaves nor flowers fade. There is Eli and Enoch yet alive without corruption. Therein groweth all manner trees and all manner trees bearing apples : therein is the tree of life. There is no passing cold nor passing heat ; but always temperate weather and air. In the middle thereof springeth a well that findeth water enough to that place ; that well is parted in four streams and rivers. The way thereto is stopped and unknown to mankind after the sin of the first man. For it is closed and beclipped all about with a fiery wall ; so that the burning thereof reacheth nigh to heaven."

St. Brendan's island, gathering around it the traditions of the Fortunate Islands, kept for centuries its place in the ocean. It was identified with Aprositus, the Unapproachable, which Ptolemy had placed near the Canaries. "There is yet another isle," says Honorius of Antun writing in the twelfth century, "the which may not be seen when men would go thereto, but some go thither as men say, and it is called the Isle Lost. This isle found Saint Brendan." Thither, as the Spaniards said, Roderick the last of the Gothic kings was transported after his defeat by the Moors, and the Portuguese made it the refuge of their own vanquished king, Sebastian. It appears in Venetian and Genoese maps of the fourteenth and fifteenth centuries and in the globe which Martin Behem constructed at Nuremberg in 1492. Columbus hoped to meet with it on his voyage. The site given to the island varied greatly ; but a mirage reflecting the coast-line of Palma placed it, in the general opinion, somewhere in the neighbourhood of the Canaries. Repeated attempts were made to discover it, the last as recently as in the year 1721.

The Mountain of Stones seems to be the fabulous mountain of adamant or loadstone which figures in the story of Sindbad. It was well known to Medieval geographers and romancers and originated probably in the fact that canoes used in the Indian Ocean were stitched together with twine made from the husk of the Indian nut. The name of the whale Jasconius is from the Irish iasc, a fish. His unsuccessful attempts to put his tail in his mouth may be due to the Norse legend of the snake Jormungandr or Midgard, the offspring of Loki, which was thrown into the sea, and encircled the whole world by putting its tail into its mouth. Honorius of Antun (translated in Caxton, Myrrour of the World) says, " In this sea of India is another fish so huge that on his back groweth earth and grass, and seemeth properly that it is a great island. Whereof it happeth sometime that the mariners sailing by the sea be greatly deceived and abused. For they ween certainly that it be firm land, wherefore they go out of their ships thereon. And when they have made to burn after their need weening to be on a firm land, in-continent as this marvellous fish feeleth the heat of the fire, he moveth him suddenly and diveth him down into the water as deep as he may. And thus all that is upon him is lost in the sea. And by this means many ships be drowned and perish, and the people when they supposed to ¡have been in safety." ¡Compare Paradise Lost, i., 200-208. With regard to the angels become birds, Dante finds spirits in the first circle of Hell who stood neutral in the great rebellion against God :

> " Angeli che non furon ribelli
> Nè fur fedeli a Dio, ma per sè foro."
>
> Inferno iii., 38-39.

" The Gryphon " (p. 65) says Bartholomew de Glanvilla, " is a beast with wings and is four-footed and breedeth in the Mountains Hyperborean. He is like to the lion in all parts of the body and to the eagle only in the head and wings : and is strong enemy to the horse. And gryphons keep the mountains in which be gems and precious stones and suffer them not to be taken from thence." (De Prop. Rer. xviii., cap. lvi.) The beautiful and touching story of Judas—retold, it will be remembered, by Matthew Arnold—has no precise parallel in Medieval literature. In the " Vision of Saint Paul," written by Adam de Ros, an Anglo-Norman trouvere, it is said that by the intercession of that Apostle and the angels, the torments of the damned are remitted every week from Saturday evening to Monday morning. The objects which surround Judas on the rock are made in the English version to point morals suggested by the life of the time ; an abuse of almsgiving when the rich seek to square their account with Heaven at the expense of their poorer brethren ; and the duty of giving to the clergy and of repairing roads, regarded in those days of difficult travelling as a pious work deserving spiritual reward. (Comp. Jusserand, English Way-faring Life in the Fourteenth Century, p. 44).

The text is an abridgment of the Latin not included in Jacobus de Voragine. Unfortunately it omits several interesting particulars. Three monks in the original join Saint Brendan at the last moment and one of them has his end in the island of the deserted hall (p. 55). The walls of the building are hung round with bridle-bits of silver, according to an Irish custom ; he steals one but Saint Brendan sees the tempter in the form of a little black boy beckoning to him, and reveals the theft. The monk confesses his fault and is absolved, but dies on the island and is taken up to heaven by angels of light. The English version mentions the prediction of Saint Brendan concerning another of the three, that he will be left on the Island of Ankers, but omits its fulfilment. It occurred soon after the voyagers had been delivered from the peril of the great fish that spouted water. They came to an island that stood on a level with the sea : and there was nothing that grew high thereon but all the earth was covered with white and purple flowers. Three troops of monks, boys in snow-white garments, young men in violet, and old men clad in purple dalmatics welcomed St. Brendan and his companions with hymns : and as they sang a bright cloud came and over-shadowed the island. Then two of the youths came and brought grapes of wondrous size and sweetness into the boat and asked that the monk might remain with them. So his companions took their farewells of him and he left them and was joyfully received. Again the monks—like Maelduin—fall in with an iceberg, or column in the waves, so high that it's top is invisible. It has a canopy like silver, while the column itself is of the clearest crystal. They sail about it for four days, and discover on the south side a chalice of the same material as the canopy and a paten of that of the column. These St. Brendan takes away, saying, "Our Lord Jesus Christ has displayed to us this marvel and has given to us two gifts therefrom as a token to others." In the Latin, the candles of the monastery church are lighted by a fiery arrow.

A manuscript in the British Museum (dated 1470) contains

Caxton's text. It is a prose rendering of a metrical version in the Harleian collection. (No. 2,270 fol. 41). Occasionally the transcriber has misread his authority, and in such instances I have not hesitated to correct the text: they are few in number and of little importance. The prose and the verse were edited together by T. Wright (St. Brendan, a medieval legend of the sea, Percy Society), reproduced as an appendix to Father O'Donoghue's *Brendaniana* (Dublin 1873). The Latin Navigatio will be found in Moran's *Acta Sancti Brendani* (Dublin 1872). O'Hanlon's *Lives of the Irish Saints*, vol. 5, contains much information relating to St. Brendan.

P. 77. St. Christopher.

July 25th. In the East, May 9th.

P. 87. St. Eustace.

September 20th. The Acts of St. Eustace are derived from the Greek of Simeon Metaphrastes, a writer of the ninth century. Few ecclesiastical historians have hesitated to treat them as fabulous. A martry of the name of Eustachius may however have suffered at Rome; for an ancient church there was dedicated to his memory and his name occurs in early calendars. The date assigned to the event is September 20th, A.D. 118. The popular legend belongs of course to a very large class of tales of similar " recognitions."

P. 102. St. George.

April 23rd. The *Golden Legend* contains the earliest extant description of St. George's combat with the dragon. It has also an abstract of the apocryphal Acts condemned by Pope Gelasins in 494 but used as material for the lections on St. George's day in the Sarum and other breviaries.

As this is tedious and of inferior interest I have preferred to let the famous allegory stand alone. For an examination of it in detail one need hardly refer to Baring Gould's *Curious Myths* and Ruskin's *St. Mark's Rest*, supplement, *The Place of Dragons*.

P. 108.   St. Giles.

September 1st.

P. 113.   St. Julian, Hospitator.

Jan. 9th.   The legend as we have it here—it is of late origin—is clearly a piece of folk lore, a variant of the tale of Ordipus and of Prince Agib, the third calendar in the *Arabian Nights.*

P. 114.   St. Katherine.

November 25th.   The mystic marriage forms no part of the earliest accounts of this saint, and it is not found in the Latin and French of the *Golden Legend.*   It was added in the English of John of Benynguay used by Caxton, probably a transcript from one of the numerous poems on the subject which were produced from the thirteenth century onward.

P. 145.   St. Margaret.

July 20th.

P. 152.   St. Sylvester.

December 21st.   The Acts of St. Sylvester, written in Greek by Simeon Metaphrastes, were Eastern in origin: perhaps their earliest form was Syriac, as a version in that language exists, belonging probably to the sixth century. They seem strangely enough to be founded on a heathen calumny.   Constantine, after the murder of his son Crispus was seized with remorse and applied to the heathen philosophers for consolation ; but they told him that there could be no expiation for such offences as his.   Then he turned to the bishops, who promised to wash away his sin on condition of repentance and baptism.   He therefore became a Christian and tried to lead others in the same way (Sozomen, Hist. Eccl. i. v.).   As a fact Constantine was not baptized till near the end of his life.   Here in germ are the leprosy (of sin) and the blood bath : and with these are mingled early traditions of great gifts of the Emperor to the church, afterwards expanded into the Donation, by which he surrendered his palace, the city of Rome and the provinces of the West to Sylvester the Catholic Pope and his successors.

P. 161. The Passion of the Eleven Thousand Virgins.

St. Ursula's Day is October 21st.

P. 166. The Seven Sleepers.

Commemorated on July 27th. These and the Eleven Thousand Virgins are very fully dealt with in Baring Gould's *Curious Myths*. The story about Edward the Confessor is from William of Malmesbury's Chronicle. ii. 13.

P. 192. St. Martha.

July 29th. From a Provençal religious romance attributed to Herbanus Maurus, Archbishop of Mainz, who died A.D. 856. The dragon, here as elsewhere, is probably derived from symbols and pictures representing the triumph of Christianity over paganism.

P. 188. St. Longinus.

March 15th. Like Veronica and Amphibalus this saint has probably derived his name from the object which figures most largely in his story; in his case the longche ($\lambda \acute{o} \gamma \chi \eta$) or spear with which he pierced the Saviour's side.

P. 193. Judas and Pilate.

The account of the youth of Judas is from an apocryphal gospel. (Thilo, Tod Apocryph. N. T. Evang. Infant. c. 35). Pilate's story is a fusion of a German legend concerning his youth and the *Mors Pilati* which gives his trial before Tiberius and the troubles which befell his remains at Mount Pilatus. (See Smith's *Dictionary of the Bible*, Articles *Judas and Pilate*.)

P. 203.   Julian the Apostate.

Julian's intercourse with the Neoplatonist and magician Maximus of Ephesus furnished the basis of this legend. The story about the sign of the cross is found in a somewhat different form in Gregory of Nazianzus. (*Orat. IV. I. contr. Julianum*, vol. I., p. 578 of his works in Migne's edition.) Flickering lights, voices and spectres encountered him as he was in a dark passage with his teacher practising unlawful arts. From old habit he made the sign of the cross and the horrible visions disappeared. Twice he was attacked again and successfully defended himself in the same way. He was puzzled at the power of the sign but was reassured by being told that the devils trembled at it because it signified something worse than themselves. The account of the supposed slayer of Julian (see Gibbon c. xxiv) is built upon a story given by John of Damascus on the authority of Helladius the disciple and successor of Basil the Great. (*De Imaginibus, Orat. I.*)

P. 206.   St. Macarius of Alexandria.

January 2nd. A hermit who lived for about sixty years in the deserts of Egypt, and died A.D. 394.

P. 209.   St. Felix.

January 14th. A native of Nola in Campaina fourteen miles from Naples, he was ordained priest about a.d. 250. He is celebrated in the poems of Paulinus, bishop of Nola (A.D. 409–431).

P. 211.   Peter the Toller.

The story is taken from the life of John the Almoner written by Simeon Metaphrastes.

P. 215.   Invention of St. Firmin.

September 25th. St. Firminus, a native of Pampeluna was the bishop and first martyr of Amiens. His death is said by the Bollandists to have occurred at the beginning of the second century. When St. Salvius was Bishop of Amiens (518–612), the resting place of his predecessor, which had been before unknown, was miraculously revealed to him as he was celebrating Mass. Then followed the translation of the remains as described in the text. Caxton took the story from his French Golden Legend (Paris, 1480), which contains several legends, not found in other editions, of Saints of Flanders and northern France. One of the portals of the north façade of Amiens Cathedral is sculptured with incidents drawn from the life of St. Firminus.

P. 218. Miracles of St. Nicholas. St. Nicholas of Myra.

December 6th. These tales concerning this most popular saint are taken from Vincent de Beauvais, "Speculum historiale."

P. 235. The Translation of St. Mark.

The Translation of St. Mark is usually said to have taken place about A.D. 815. The body was supposed to have been deposited for greater security under one of the great pillars of the Church of St. Mark in Venice. (*Daru. Histoire de Venise I.* 57.)

P. 243. St. Anastasia.

December 25th. A lady of Illyricum burned in the Island of Palmarola in the Tyrrhenian Sea about A.D. 304, during the persecution of Diocletian.

P. 254. St. John the Almoner.

January 23rd. Catholic Patriarch of Alexandria, A.D. 609–616.

P. 258. St. Genevieve.

January 3rd. Died probably about A.D. 512. This virgin through her reputation for holy living obtained such influence with Clovis that she succeeded in softening the rigours of the Frankish conquest and was afterwards honoured as the patroness of Paris.

P. 265. St. Patrick's Purgatory was a celebrated resort of Pilgrims from the twelfth to the fourteenth century. There was a monastery on an island in Lough Derg in county Donegal : and hard by was a cave which had a gate always closed of which the abbot kept the keys. That was the entranec into Purgatory which had been revealed to the Apostle of Ireland. It first became widely known in the twelfth century. Giraldus Cambrensis in his *Topographica Hibernica* written about 1188 says that the island is divided into two parts, one containing a church of exceeding sanctity, the other wholly abandoned to demons. From his time onward it was visited by many, often persons of great distinction, as we know by safe conducts granted by the king for the purpose. After permission obtained and due religious preparation the gate was unbarred and the pilgrim spent the night within the cave. Some descriptions of the gruesome sights to be met with there, especially that known as the Vision of Sir Owayne had a wide popularity. Froisart mentions the visit of a knight to the cave, who however saw but little. In 1497 the Pope satisfied himself that the claims of St. Patrick's Purgatory were unfounded and ordered it to be destroyed. In a short time Pilgrims again resorted thither ; and, although a law forbidding these visits was passed in the second year of Queen Anne, they have continued down to recent times. See Baring-Gould's *Curious Myths* and T. Wright's *St. Patrick's Purgatory* (London 1844.)

The Vision of Tundale is not strictly an account of a visit to the cave on the Island at all. Tundale was a nobleman of Cashel, who lavished his money in vain-glory instead of bestowing it on the church and the poor. He was stricken into a trance which lasted from Wednesday till Saturday. The sights which befell him were not very different from those in the vision given in the text : the bridge invariably appears in these stories. The date of his vision is about 1149 and accounts of it were circulated in Latin and French and in English verse.